Lock Down Publications and Ca$h Presents

THE GIRLRILLA AND HER N*GGA *KAY-O*

Written By
CHRISTOPHER "DIESEL" HORNEZES

CHRISTOPHER "DIESEL" HORNEZES

Lock Down Publications
P.O. Box 944
Stockbridge, GA 30281
www.lockdownpublications.com

Like our page on Facebook: Lock Down Publications
www.facebook.com/lockdownpublications.ldp

Stay Connected with Us!

Text **LOCKDOWN** to 22828 to stay up-to-date with new releases, sneak peaks, contests and more…

Like our page on Facebook:
Lock Down Publications

Join Lock Down Publications/The New Era Reading Group

Visit our website:
www.lockdownpublications.com

Follow us on Instagram:
Lock Down Publications

Email Us: We want to hear from you!

Acknowledgements/Shoutouts

I don't think I'll ever be able to understand why so many people hate on others.

Insecurity? Stupidity? They're just lame? Who knows, and who cares? All of you clownz that I see every day that just stare at me when I walk past then look away when I look to see what you're looking at… keep on watching a successful man of color do his thing, while ya keep your *Bad Girls Club* thing going. I'm gonna keep writing novels and worry about me. God had my back. Get a life, yo. Real rap.

Shoutout to Ca$h, LDP, everyone dropping hits under Lockdown Publications! Shoutout to my family! Shoutout to everyone that had motivated me! Chino Dre! Camo! Jose! Rojo! Tino! Shoutout to everyone buying my books! I love y'all, yo! Real rap! Thank all of you for your support. I'ma keep 'em coming too.

R.I.P. to my brothers, Booty Moe of North Chicago and Fonzo of Zion. Shoutout to Gone-But-Not-Forgotten at all PJ! To my mother, Christina Hornezes, R.I.P. To my dad, Tommy Royster, R.I.P, and my g-ma, Louise Hornezes, R.I.P. I love and miss y'all.

Lastly, to my new friend, Marissa, keep ya head up, Ma. You got this. To my homie, Mattie, mad luv to you for withal you've done for me. I will never forget it.

Introduction

"Ryan!"

"Bitch, what the fuck you want, yo?" Ryan snapped, glaring at his girlfriend, Macie, while he put another rubber band around another ten-thousand-dollar stack of big faces.

"Nigga, don't get slapped!" she shot back, stomping toward him angrily in her thigh-high Louboutin stiletto boots that matched her denim Balenciaga shoulder-less dress. "I asked you a muthafuckin' question! Answer me!"

In their luxurious home in the Monroeville area of Pittsburgh, Ryan was counting up the cash of his re-up in the big gourmet-style kitchen when his chick marched her ass in and started fucking with his mental.

"I already told you, Mace! She won't find out! Now, shut the fuck up and get outta my kitchen!"

"Ryan, Kayla is not stupid! She will find out! She found out ya mans, Slug, was stealin' from her and look what happened to him!"

Ryan looked up at Macie. "Slug went M.I.A., yo."

"Exactly! And who you think made him go there, nigga?"

"Sorry, Ryan is not there at the moment. Please leave a message at the beep."

Macie put her hand on her hip. "Uh huh. Where's the beep?"

"Ain't no beep! Now go somewhere, man! Damn! Crybaby ass!"

"You know what?" Macie chuckled. "You wanna play games wit' her, right? Then, you take ya' muthafuckin' weight when she comes for you! Dumbass nigga!" Macie marched out of the kitchen then.

"Fuck outta here, yo. Homiez, a nigga that's scared of a bitch is a whole schmuck," Ryan said to himself then grabbed his phone and put on some music.

Hardo's *Fame Or Feds* started playing. Ryan nodded his head and rapped along with the words, putting another stack of cash into the money counter.

Just then, Tez, Jay, and Real walked in with bookbags and duffel bags stuffed with cash.

"What up, cutty?" Tez spoke, dapping Ryan up then Jay and Real.

"Shit. Tryna hurry up and get the fuck outta here before my whinin' ass bitch comes back," Ryan told him, as the three set the bags on the hardwood top of the center island that he was sitting at.

They laughed.

"What's the problem now?" asked Jay.

"She think a nigga supposed to be scared of Kayla."

They stopped laughing. Ryan looked at them. He shook his head.

"Y'all niggas is pathetic, yo. Homiez."

"Maaan, yo, look. Kayla is not no ordinary bitch, cutty," Real spoke up. "I'm keepin' it a buck when I say this, but toyin' wit' her money is playin' wit' ya life. And if you ain't scared of her... then you must not know her homie, O. Dude is a muh'fuckin' killa for real, cuz."

Ryan stood up then. He walked toward Real, staring daggers into his eyes. Tez and Jay stepped back and got ready to enjoy the show. The look in Ryan's eyes was common when he was on it.

"Aye! Ryan! Yo, my nigga, ch..."

Crack! Crack! Wham!

Ryan pieced Real up with a hot 'n spicy three-piece that made him fly backwards and land hard on the floor.

"Soft ass nigga! You scared of a bitch! A little ass bitch at that! Nigga, get the fuck outta my crib!"

"Bro, you buggin', my nigga!" Real replied with a sore jaw. "I'm only sayin', cuz, that if we goin' jump on wit' that nigga, Tuck, we can't just think Kayla gon' be the type to let it ride!"

"Man, fuck that bitch and her *girlrilla* mob or whatever the fuck they is! That bitch bleed like every other bitch tryna be tough!"

"True, but I bet it ain't gon' be me that you make bleed, bitch ass nigga."

Ryan immediately looked up from Real and gasped when he saw who had just said that. Tez and Jay were both dumbfounded, eyes bugged wide like dinner plates. Real rolled onto his side and looked up. When he saw Kayla there in the flesh with her all-female mob of money-getting killers, his heart started beating like a subwoofer with a Twista song thumping through it.

Kayla glared angrily at Ryan, ignoring his groupies. At her side was her slightly older cousin, Shayla, better known as Shay. Behind her and Shay were Chante, Jerrica, and Valerie. The three gripped fully automatic Dracos with one-hundred-round drums. Shay gripped two automatic Glock 9s with mini-fifty-round drums locked in, while Kayla wore leather gloves over her hands with nothing in them.

"So, you got plans to join the losin' team, huh, Ryan?" Kayla asked, looking at the Notorious B.I.G. sized Ryan.

"I'm s-sayin', Kayla!" Ryan barked, stammering at the same time. "Niggaz is tryna eat like you are! How you the only one touchin' millions, and we only getting a few hunnid gees? That ain't cool, yo!"

Kayla shook her head. "You know what else ain't cool, Ryan? Bein' a clown that steal from the chick that has you livin' in this big ass crib and pushin' a new G-Wagen. Shame on you."

The second she finished speaking, Ryan heard the tapping of high heels. He saw Macie appear, then in her hands, she held the handles of two red Louis Vuitton bags. Ryan's eyes went wide then filled with rage from the betrayal of his own bitch, who he flossed out and had living with him in his miniature mansion; he went ballistic.

"Bitch! You set me up! I'm break ya fuckin' neck, yo! Homiez, I'ma kill you!"

"Shut the fuck up, you clown ass nigga," Macie shot back, dropping the bags by Shay's feet. "I told ya stupid ass that she was gon' find out. I just didn't tell you that I was gon' be the one to tell her."

Infuriated, Ryan charged like an angry bull being teased with a red banner. He was so focused on strangling Macie that by the time he saw Kayla's swift move, it was too late. Kayla pulled out the razor sharpened machete that she had concealed down the side of her sweats and swung it at Ryan's face. The blade sliced right into the side of his mouth, cutting right through the jaw muscle at his left. Ryan screamed in pain. Kayla snatched her cutter out of his face, and he dropped to the floor, bleeding heavily from the deep cut. She raised the machete up and hacked at his left shoulder, slicing clean through it, severing his arm from his body.

"Get his arm, Macie," she demanded over the bloodcurdling scream that filled the kitchen.

Obeying her, Macie went and grabbed the severed limb by the hand. Kayla hacked Ryan's right arm off next. Blood spewed out all over the floor. She made Macie grab his right arm and hold it, then she kicked Ryan in his head, making him flip over. Standing directly over him, Kayla again raised the blade up high.

"Kayla! Nooo!"

Whack!

She brought the machete down on the center of his head, chopping down through his skull to his brain. Ryan's body jerked then went limp. She snatched the blade out and wiped his blood on his Balmain shirt. Looking at Ryan's guys, she saw they were all staring at her, dumbfounded.

"Grab my money, take it out to my girls' whip. Now," she told them, and they immediately did as told with Chante, Jerrica, and Valerie escorting them.

"Daaaaayuuum, yo! Aye, yous a girlrilla for real, like they say! Heeeey! Hooo! Heeey!" Macie sang then started twerking her ass.

"For someone that's just as guilty as Ryan is, you sure are actin' like you ain't in violation too, yo!" Shay said to her.

"Wait... What?" said Macie, abruptly pausing her twerk off.

Crack!

Kayla swung on Macie and rocked her jaw, breaking it with one punch. Macie flew into the refrigerator door, smacking into it hard. Kayla grabbed her before she fell to the ground and slammed her face into the Sub-Zero's stainless door until it was smashed in, and Macie was bleeding profusely.

Chante, Jerrica, and Valerie returned with Tez, Jay, and Real. The three saw Macie laid out with her face smashed in. They all knew that spending stolen money was just as bad as stealing it.

"Y'all niggaz want a job workin' for me?" Kayla asked them with a smirk on her face.

"Yes!" they shouted in unison, too terrified to say no.

"Too bad," Kayla replied and laughed, as Chante, Jerrica, and Valerie blew their legs off then put hot ones in their arms, immobilizing them.

Kayla ignored their bloodcurdling cries of pain, went to the stove, and turned on all the burners so that only gas fumes seeped out.

"Kayla! Please!" cried Tez, as the fumes grew stronger and stronger by the second.

She gave no reply, nor did her girls. Shay got a jug of vegetable oil from the cabinet and poured it all over Tez, Jay, and Real, while Kayla grabbed a roll of aluminum foil from a drawer. As quickly as she could, she ripped big pieces, balled them up, and tossed them into the microwave, hitting the popcorn button when she slammed the door shut.

The five ladies hauled ass up out of Ryan's house, making it to where Chante's new Ultramarine Black, 2024 Aston Martin DBX 707 truck sat parked a few houses down, away from the lit streetlights that lined the cul-de-sac that Ryan and Macie lived on.

Booom!

The house exploded, sending a gigantic fireball up into the dark sky, while the blast shook the ground. Chante slammed her Aston Martin truck in drive, mashed the gas, and tore up out of the cul-de-sac before any of the rudely awakened residents could even look out of their windows to see what the hell had just happened.

Chapter 1

Down in Homewood, where all five of them grew up, Chante dropped off Kayla and Shay at Kayla's crib up on Blackadore Avenue, across the street from a hillside cemetery and a big auto scrap shop. Kayla's single-level house was a deluxe five bedroom with the luxuries of a mansion inside, all wrapped up in cream-colored stones with glossy hardwood trim and a two-car wide asphalt driveway that led up to a built-in two car garage.

Dismissing her girls to take the money to Chante's house to get wrapped and ready to deliver to Omar, Kayla and Shay went to hop into Kayla's two-tone gray and black 2025 Rolls Royce Cullinan Mansory edition sitting on blacked-out twenty-four-inch Mansory wheels. Kayla started up the big V12 engine then pulled out of her driveway, heading up Blackadore to Mount Carmel to take it to Lincoln-Larimer and out to East Liberty to pick up the last of the cash to add to her big monthly re-up.

**

Coming up on Mellon Street, Kayla turned off of East Liberty Boulevard and rolled down the small street lined with houses and two-family apartments. She reached the three-story apartment building that was just three houses away from where Mellon crossed Hays Street. She parked in front and saw lights on inside through the first-floor apartment's living room window.

Grabbing her Glock 21, she tucked it into her sweats and fixed her hoodie's hem over it. Shay tucked one of her Glock 9s after putting a thirty-round clip in. Together, they got out and entered the front yard. Music was bumping way too loudly from inside for Kayla's liking. Loud music drew attention, and a stash house did not need attention.

"These niggaz is dumb, yo. Homiez, we need to put they asses back on the street," Shay told Kayla after she used her key to unlock the main front door.

"Noted," Kayla replied, as the music got louder when they stepped into the dark carpeted foyer area.

At the apartment's door, Shay inserted her key into the top lock and unlocked it then went to turn the knob when, suddenly, the door was yanked open, and a pair of gloved hands grabbed her and snatched her inside.

"Shayla!" Kayla shouted, whipping her gun out and rushing in after her.

Wham!

The second she entered the apartment, a hard object slammed into the left side of her head, knocking her sideways to the floor. A heavy body pounced on her and held her down. Fighting back, Kayla tried to buck the nigga up off of her, but he was more than double her size and weight.

A pair of legs connected to Timberland booted feet came into her line of sight. Kayla looked up at the man they belonged to. She went wide-eyed with shock when she saw her best friend's number one enemy there with a big grin on his face.

"What up, Kayla? Long time no see," Tuck spoke. "I been hearin' a lot 'bout ya lil girlrilla gang clique. Got niggaz shook out here. Homiez, I'm proud of y'all, but now, that shit's over wit', yo." He then gestured for her to look beyond him. Kayla saw Rob, Thuggin', Khalil, and Yuri tied up and bloody on the floor by the entryway to the kitchen. She then saw her cousin being held in a headlock by a huge man that looked like a Black Sumo wrestler. "Now check it out," Tuck continued. "I know how you get down, and I respect it. Niggaz around the hood call you the Girlrilla," Tuck chuckled. "But nonetheless, tonight, you gon' learn that I ain't playin' no games at all."

Kayla saw him turn to the three goons that stood over her four guys, each of them holding Tech 9s with cooler kits and silencers. He gave them the word, and without hesitation, they took aim at Rob, Thuggin, Khalil, and Yuri and blew them down. Tuck then looked at the giant that had Shay hemmed up. He nodded his head at the man.

"Wait! No!" Kayla screamed out.

Crack!

As if it were a twig, the giant snapped Shay's neck with one hard twist. Kayla screamed, crying her cousin's name out, as Shay's lifeless body dropped to the floor.

"Shaaylaaa, nooo!"

Smack!

"Bitch! Stop screamin'!" the man holding her yelled after he smacked the fuck out of her.

Tuck came back to her side. He told the guy to get up off her. He obeyed Tuck's command, but as soon as he did, Kayla jumped up and tried to rush Tuck.

Boc! Boc! Boc!

"Aaaaaahhhhhh!" Kayla screamed when three shots slammed into her left leg and her thigh.

She fell to the floor, screaming in pain, clutching her leg which bled profusely. Tuck stepped up to her and kicked her hard in her face, then in her stomach, and then in her leg.

"You's a dumb bitch. You know that? Just dumb." Tuck hawked a loogie in her face then kicked her once more. "Tonight, you get to live – at least until the next time we meet or if you decide to kill yaself from seein' images of my nigga breakin' ya cousin's neck in front of ya eyes. Her death is on your hands. Tell that bitch ass nigga, Omar, I said hi, and I'll be seein' him too, real soon."

With that, Tuck and his crew left out, taking bags of cash, ten bricks of cocaine, and some guns. Kayla, in agonizing pain, crawled over to her cousin. She tried to shake her awake, but Shay was gone.

Bursting into tears, Kayla cried her eyes out for her big cousin. They had been more like sisters than cousins. At thirty years of age, Shay was two years older than Kayla. After Kayla's parents were killed by a drunk driver when she was barely five years old, Shay's mother, who was Kayla's aunt, and Shay's father took Kayla in and treated her like she was their daughter, showering her with love. But Kayla and Shay fell in love with the streets. As they got older – and once they met Omar and his homies – the fast life became what they wanted, and they relied on Omar to teach them all about it. He did so, to the best of his ability.

***

Kayla heard glass breaking just then. She hurried and turned just in time to see that a Molotov cocktail had been thrown into the apartment through the window. Flames quickly spread when the glass bottle shattered on the floor.

"Shit!" Kayla panicked, as flames raced to take over the whole apartment.

Desperate to live, she dragged herself toward the door, just making it as the fire reached the big HDTV and doubled from the electrical power source. She grabbed the door handle and pulled herself up. Opening the door, she hobbled out of the burning apartment to the building's front door. She made it out just as an older Chevy Tahoe peeled off from next to her Rolls Royce truck.

She then noticed the flames dancing around inside of her $620,000 whip. Gasping, Kayla's heart dropped when it exploded, setting off two more explosions from the two cars it was parked in between. Kayla looked up toward the end of Mellon and caught a glimpse of the Tahoe bend the corner onto East Liberty Avenue, disappearing from her line of sight.

"I swear to God. Homiez, on my dead mother and father, I'm gonna catch that nigga and make him eat pieces of himself," Kayla growled, then hobbling, she hurried to get up out of there before fire crews and cops could show up to get to a phone and call the only other person in the world besides Shay that she could depend on no matter what he was doing.

***

YFN Lucci's *Wet* with Big Latto bumped from the expensive home audio system in his luxurious and spacious master bedroom. His eyes rolled to the back of his head as the sensational pleasure from the dark- chocolate freak's phenomenal oral skills made his toes curl up. Laid back against his pillows, he enjoyed the neck she was giving him, putting her all into it like she always did.

She was a stallion, no lie, with her beautiful dark skin tone and her long, black tresses hanging loosely down her bare shoulders. Her big breasts were plump and succulent. She had a slim waist, cute face, wide hips, and a fat ass that he couldn't wait to watch jiggle, while he hit it from the back. She aimed to please him any time he wanted. Nothing was off limits, just how he liked his shmutts.

Yajaira deep throated as much of his thick, ten-inch dick as she could while hunched over, tooting her juicy fifty-inch ass up in the air. She was aiming to make Omar cum so hard that he went numb for a minute. He had that bag, and she wanted some of the big faces inside of it.

She released his cock from her mouth. Gripping it at the base, she spit on it, then slowly, she licked it back up before she ran her tongue down the side of his shaft to his balls. He groaned as she sucked his nuts, using a hand to jerk his dick at the same time. His cock swelled up in her mouth. She tasted pre-cum a second later. She took his dick out of her mouth, and right as Latto's *Brokey* came on, she changed positions and got on all fours, looking back at Omar with lust and fiery desire.

Omar's eyes went as big as her fat, juicy, chocolate bubble when she went face down, ass up for him. Eager to crack from the back, Omar got up and scooted up behind her. He grabbed her ass, smacking it. She made it wiggle, teasing him with her plump-ass money maker. He grabbed his hardness and slid it inside of her tight, wet pussy, gritting his teeth, as her walls enveloped him welcomingly.

"Oooohhh, shit, Omar! Oooo!" Yajaira cried out, as he pounded her hard and fast.

Omar went savage on her. He grabbed her hair with his left hand and fucked the fuck out of her. She cried out his name repeatedly, begging him not to stop. He felt her clenching around him, the pussy getting wetter and wetter, her moaning getting louder and louder.

Minutes later, Yajaira exploded. She came all over his dick and thighs, drenching him. Not done with her yet, Omar pulled his wet dick out of her, grabbed her cheeks, and spread them. He spit a wad of saliva onto her puckered brown eye, then he smeared it all around with his cock. Omar put the bulbous tip to it and eased inside of her back door.

Yajaira squealed in delight, as she felt his joint enter her asshole. It was that superfreak shit that she loved, being dominated by a rich, hood ass nigga like the golden-fried chicken complected, braided up goon behind her. Just looking at him could make her climax. She compared Omar to the criminal turned model Jeremy Meeks, but he was hood as fuck with a bank account that looked like a phone number and a wallet that looked like a Bible.

Omar was that nigga, and she wanted to be that bitch, but Yajaira knew and hated the fact that he wasn't the type to commit. Plus, she despised his home girl. It seemed like the girl always called when they were busy, and Omar never hesitated to go running to her like a trained dog. Nonetheless, Yajaira played her position – a shameless freak in his sheets and a bad bitch in the streets that all the dope boys wanted to get at but couldn't because she belonged to Omar.

"Oohh, ssshhhit!" Omar shouted right as she felt his nut coming.

He pulled his dick out and skeeted globs of hot cum all in her ass crack, while she held her cheeks apart. He jerked his cock until it was empty, and her crack was full.

"Wooo!" Omar took a deep breath in and exhaled, while Yajaira giggled at him, turning on her side to face him.

"Bae, we goin' shoppin' tomorrow still, right?" she asked right as Omar's iPhone started ringing. "Maaan, come on now, yo!" she whined when he went to grab it.

"Shhh!" Omar silenced her, then seeing it was his right hand hitting his line, he immediately answered. "Yello!"

Yajaira curled her lip up, as she sat next to him. Looking at him, she saw his expression go from "I just got some *bomb*-ass pussy" to "Somebody bout to die!"

"I'm on the way! Stay low! I'm comin' right now!" he spoke with such urgency that Yajaira grew alarmed.

Omar jumped off the bed.

"O? What happened, bae? Where is you goin'?" she asked, but he didn't answer.

He quickly got dressed in the same clothes that she had stripped him out of.

"O?" she called again, hopping off the bed to go to him.

"I gotta go handle somethin', yo! Chill!" he snapped, putting his blue Timberlands back on then grabbing his Desert Eagle .40 out of his nightstand drawer.

He headed toward the door.

"Uh uh! Hell no, nigga!" Yajaira followed him, pissed as shit. "Omar! You said we was goin' shoppin'! Together!"

He got to the door and opened it. Yajaira screamed as his two solid smokey-bluish gray able Blood Cane Corsos ran into the room, looking like giant pit bulls, with pointed, clipped ears, huge heads, and muscular bodies, growling viciously at her. They both ran up on her, ready to rip her to pieces. Yajaira attempted to swat them like a damn fool.

"Smoke! Haze! Back!" Omar commanded the two brutes. They obeyed although clearly reluctantly.

"Yajaira. These dogs have the second most strongest bite of all dog breeds known to man and are descendants of ancient war dogs. Do you want to become their next meal?" Omar asked, looking at her like she was just dumb as fuck.

"No, Omar! I just want to spend time with you! You always rushin' off for some bullshit!"

Omar stepped to her, glaring down into her eyes. "My people ain't bullshit, bitch! Watch ya mouth, or you will be food! Clean this mufucka up by the time I get back. Get stupid if you want! They will keep ya' ass in line while I'm gone."

He ushered his dogs out the bedroom, closed the door on her, then ran out of the house to his new obsidian black, 2025, Overfinch edition Range Rover P615 and jumped in. Frantically, he peeled off from his enormous home, leaving the upscale Plum neighborhood to get to his homegirl.

Chapter 2

Omar pushed his Rover to the limit. He sped his ass all the way out East Liberty. He arrived at a big Home Depot where she was to be waiting for him. When he saw her emerge from a cut by the garden center entrance, limping and obviously in agonizing pain, Omar jumped out of his car.

"Kay!" he shouted, running to her, scared but relieved that she was alive.

She was bloody. The cloth wrapped around her leg was crimson. He was horrified to see his homegirl like that.

"I'm cool, O!" Kayla wept. "Just get me outta here, man!"

He scooped her up, ran her to his SUV, and put her in the front. Jumping behind the wheel, he dipped off, making a call as he headed toward Homewood.

"Yo, Doc! Kayla's shot! I'm enroute! Less than ten away!" he told the hood doctor that was on his payroll then ended the call. "Hold on, Kay! You gon' be aight! My word, yo!" Omar swore, as he held her hand, feeling how weak her grip felt.

He hurried up Frankstown Street, and getting to Blackadore Road, he arrived at the old jitney cab station owned by the doctor. Omar skidded to a stop in front of it. The old African doctor and his surgeon wife came out. Hopping out of the SUV, Omar raced to get his best friend from diaper days out and into the makeshift operating room inside.

"We got 'ha, Omar," Doctor Oswego told him. "Do not worry, my friend."

19

Omar kissed Kayla's forehead then stepped away from the table where she laid. She looked at him with puffy, red eyes as he stepped back. She could see the fires of hell burning in his.

Just as he stepped out, fatigue set in, and before she could call out to him... everything went dark.

***

"Yeah, what up, cutty?" answered Ace.

"Aye, yo! Kayla got hit up by that punk ass, bitch ass nigga, Tuck, bruh!" Omar told his right hand.

"On the dead homiez, cuz, I'm ready! You already know! Lil sis is my people, yo!"

"I'm already knowin', bruh. I'm at Oswego's; I can't leave 'til I got her with me."

"Say less. I can go grab the squad, an' we can start a few fires since dude wants some shmoke, cuz."

"I want you to burn his whole crew up but hold off. I'm just lettin' you know, so at a moment's notice, we ridin' on them niggaz."

"Aight. Yo, tell sis I love her, cutty, when the doc put her back on her feet," Ace requested.

"Yup. One, my nigga."

"One."

Omar ended the call then. He took a deep breath, trying to calm himself. He was so close to losing control and pressing the button on everyone associated with Tuck – friends, family, homies, connections. Nobody was off limits.

"This nigga gon' wish he came out his mother a plain ass boy, yo," Omar said, as a million ways to execute revenge for Kayla filled his mind.

***

A few hours later, Omar was awakened by the sound of Doctor Oswego's voice.

"Oma'," the man called to him.

Omar hopped up before he even opened his eyes.

"Yeah? How is she, Doc?" he pleaded to know.

"She is doing well. I repai'd all 'de wounds 'ahnd stitched ha' up. The gun shots were 'troo 'ahnd 'troos. She will be very sore for a few days, weeks. She must rest though, Oma'."

"Okay! So, she's good?"

Doctor Oswego nodded. "Yes, but 'dis is 'de fourth time I have treated ha' for bullet wounds. Next time, she may not be so lucky. Ya' need to keep her away from 'de gunplay, son."

In no way, shape, or form was Omar confident that he could do that. Kayla was as hood as it got for a lady. She loved getting money, fighting, and playing with guns. She was as much of a goon as Omar was. He and every real nigga out there knew that you could take a chick out of the hood, but you could not take the hood out of a chick.

"Can I see her?" Omar asked.

"You can take ha' home, but ya must make sure 'de girl does not ova' exert haself, Oma'. Do ya' hear me?"

Omar nodded then followed the doctor to where his wife was just finishing wrapping Kayla's leg and thigh. Her sweats had been removed and covering her was a hospital gown. He ran right to her side and wrapped her up in his arms.

"Goddamn, Kayla! Yo, what the fuck, Ma! You dun damn near gave a nigga a heart attack, yo! What the hell happened?"

Kayla suddenly burst into tears. Omar held her, trying his best to comfort her. Kayla crying was a rare phenomenon. He knew it was likely way worse than what was already known, and it was confirmed when she told him about Shay.

21

When Kayla told him that Tuck was responsible, it threw him for a loop. The last he knew, the man had just up and disappeared. Popping back up was one thing but having been the one responsible for Shay's death... Omar was livid.

It had been nearly twenty years ago that Kayla had jumped off of the porch with her cousin. Kayla had been a tomboy type of kid. Omar had been her homie from an even earlier age, and as he grew, learning the street life, so did she and Shay. He groomed them and kept them safe. What he learned, he taught them, and they had gotten a vicious rep around the hood by the time they entered their teens.

Kayla and Omar were quickly becoming known as Kay-O by all who tried them. They came as hard as a right hook and were a knockout that nobody could get up from when they struck. Things slightly changed as Kayla began developing into a woman. She grew breasts, wide hips, and a jaw-dropping fat ass with thick thighs and runner legs to match. Her buttery-brown skin tone and her long, silky hair gave her an exotic look.

To the current day, she stood 5'6", voluptuous yet athletic, with flawless natural beauty. Her hazel eyes were walnut shaped and set under perfectly arched eyebrows. Her hair had been dyed from its natural dark brown color to a rich golden honey brown. She kept a diamond stud in her right nostril, and she had juicy lips that drew stares from everyone.

With the body of a goddess and the beauty of a top model, Kayla turned heads as if she was a fat, juicy steak, and everyone was starving. Even in jeans, sweats, t-shirts, Jordans, Air Forces, and Tims, Kayla had more eyes on her than the chicks that popped out in tight dresses and heels. She stayed strapped and always ready to kick the fair one with a bitch or a nigga without any hesitation.

Omar often joked with her and said Kayla was like the singing phenom SZA but had that tough girl swag like GloRilla. Kayla took it as a compliment because they were the baddest chicks in the entertainment industry, and

22

GloRilla was a big fan of the Pittsburgh Steelers, just like Kayla was.

"I should've been faster, Omar!" Kayla cried in his arms. "She was my blood, man! I failed her!"

"Naw, baby girl. You didn't fail. It's just... went really wrong. Don't blame yaself though, yo. Homiez, this ain't on you. That nigga, Tuck, gon' get it, Kay. I swear that to you, Ma. I may not be blood, but you know y'all always have me. No matter what. I love you, Kay."

Kayla sobbed in his arms, though his words brought her great comfort. Omar meant the world to her. They were homies. Friends to the end. Though virtually everyone in and out of their circle thought they were made for each other, they denied it, but they were both horrible liars when it came to the attraction they had for each other.

"I love you too, O," Kayla replied, as her soul cried over the loss of her big cousin, but her tears were mixed with those of true joy from being wrapped up safely in Omar's arms again.

***

Chante, Jerrica, and Valerie were outside of Omar's house when he pulled up. The three were posted up next to Chante's Cadillac truck. As soon as Omar pulled into the driveway, they ran up to his car, nearly yanking the passenger's door open before he even came to a stop.

"Kay, oh, my God!" Chante cried, hugging Kayla like a worried, sick sister, while her other two homegirls did their best to contain their grief. "Yo, what the hell happened, girl?"

Kayla explained it all. Omar listened and felt his anger soaring. He was unable to process Shay being left like that. He was aware that the ladies all knew the risks of being knee-deep in the game, but still, he was raised to have more compassion for women than most other men.

"On everything I love, cuz," said Jerrica, pounding her open left hand with her fist, "them niggaz is dead, yo! On the Homiez! Let's go!"

"Jerrica," Omar called to her.

The three looked into the car. Omar looked at Jerrica, her deep rich auburn hair in two braids to the back, which went well with her rich dark chocolate skin tone. Chante was butter toffee complexioned with dark brown roots that turned mahogany down toward her ass. Valerie was light bronze and had an exotic look with dark, wavy hair, compliments of her mixed Black, German, and Cherokee heritage, and she stayed quiet as the boss spoke. Kayla looked over at him herself, trying to stay focused on the matter at hand… not the unbelievably handsome and rich dope man next to her.

"Believe me, we gon' get all them bitch ass niggaz, but they're expectin' immediate retaliation," Omar said.

Jerrica sighed. She already knew that but was so fired up about Shay that she didn't give a fuck. She was ready to charge full speed ahead.

"So, what we supposed to do, O?" Chante asked with her hands on her hips. "Sit and wait like we scared?"

"Yeah, O. Kay just lost her cousin cause bitch niggaz can't get they own money, yo," Valerie chimed in.

"Naw. What we do is give Shay a proper burial as well as our other comrades," Omar told them all. "Then, we make sure Kayla gets back on her feet. Then, we catch that nigga, Tuck, and torture that pussy muthafucka. But Kayla delivers his death. Until then though, any motherfucking body that means anything to him dies – very painfully."

"Then, we chop his legs, and dick, and all his hands off," Chante said with the most demented look in her eyes.

"And his lips and tongue!" Jerrica added. "Fuck it! His ears too!"

"I'ma cut that nigga's heart out like them Aztec people did for that sun god they worshipped, yo!" Valerie added.

"Well, damn!" Omar's eyebrows furrowed, as he looked at the ladies, all looking like little devilettes. "What happened to just puttin' some hot ones in a nigga and movin' on?"

"Naw, yo. That's for when a clown step on our toes," Kayla spoke. "I got somethin' for dude when I catch him. Homiez, yo."

Omar looked at her. She looked evil, like her little devil horns would soon emerge, and she'd fly off to go take Tuck to the fiery depths of hell.

"Oh… okay." Omar just nodded and let it be.

"Come on, Kay. Let's get you up outta here, cuz," Chante spoke up. "O, we got it from here, cutty," she told him, attempting to help Kayla out of his car.

"Hell naw! Kayla is not leavin' my sight, yo! Homiez!" Omar declared, stopping her immediately.

"Whoa, calm down, bro. Ain't nobody tryna steal ya woman, cuz." Jerrica stepped up, defending Chante.

"Jerri!" Kayla snapped, while the others all burst out laughing. "Yo, Homiez, even wit' three bullet holes in my leg, we'll still kick the fair one, and I'll beat cha ass!"

Omar started laughing.

"You're touchy as hell. We out," Chante announced then hugged Kayla, kissing her forehead. "We got that money too, yo."

"Put it up. Shit's shut down 'til things cool off," Kayla instructed.

Nodding, Chante, Jericca, and Valerie all hugged and kissed their friend then Omar. They hopped back into the 'Lac truck and headed off.

***

At his house, Omar carried Kayla in his arms to the front door. Smoke and Haze greeted him excitedly when he entered. They went even wilder with glee when they saw Kayla.

"Smokey! Haze! Heey, babies!" cooed Kayla, patting both of their heads, receiving emphatic dog kisses from each of them in return.

"O?"

Omar heard Yajaira call out to him, as he watched his dogs get wooed by Kayla. He sucked his teeth, suddenly despising the fact that she was in his crib without bite marks all over.

Kayla stood then. "Maaan, why you bring me here when you got ya lil shmutt bucket here, yo?"

Just then, Yajaira appeared at the edge of the loft-style upper floor. Omar looked up and saw her scowling at Kayla.

"For real though? You brought her here, O?"

"Bitch, this my crib! Say somethin' crazy and you can get out! Try me!" Omar dared.

Kayla smirked at her, loving the defeated look in her eyes. She waved Omar off then marched away, pissed.

"Thot-ass bitch," Omar muttered. Turning to Kayla, he then asked, "You hungry?"

"Maan… I am starvin', yo. I feel like I been blazin' nolya all day and got the munchies bad!"

"Aight, cool. I got'chu," he said and went to scoop her up again.

"O, come on, man. I can walk," Kayla told him.

"So? Me too but I'm still carryin' you to the kitchen." He stood in front of her. "Hop on, punk."

Kayla smiled and did as he told her. She hopped onto his back and screamed when he rushed off like a linebacker toward the chef's style kitchen.

***

Later in the evening, Kayla woke up to the sounds of yelling, screaming, and vicious barking.

"Bitch! Get the fuck out!" came Omar's voice.

"Fuck you, nigga! I'm not goin' no muthafuckin' where! You just wanna fuck that ugly ass ho you say is just 'ya friend'!"

Kayla started giggling. She then heard the girl scream louder.

"*Oooowww!* Omar! He bit meee!"

Kayla hopped off the bed to see what the hell was going on. The second her feet hit the floor, pain exploded in her leg. She shrieked from the painful jolt and collapsed to the floor, crying in agony. The door to the bedroom burst open seconds later. Omar saw her on the floor and rushed to her with his dogs trailing.

"Kayla! What is you doin'?" he asked, lifting her up and setting her back on the bed where Smoke and Haze jumped on too.

"I was gon' come help you," Kayla told him, eyes still squeezed shut from how bad her leg hurt.

He grabbed the bottle of Percocet and got one out for her. Kayla popped it then washed it down with the bottle of Fiji water that had been with the Percs. The dogs both whimpered, sensing her pain.

"Don't worry about me, Kay," Omar told her. "I can handle a lil' goofy ass bitch by myself."

She chuckled. "Oh, so now she's not ya girl, huh? Cause you mad at her?"

"She was never my girl, just a bitch with a deep throat, wet pussy, and a phat ass with empty pockets."

"What did you actually see in her that made you bring her to your main house instead of that thot motel?"

Omar smiled mischievously. "She had that 'good pussy' stand."

"That what?!"

"You ain't never saw how some bitches got a certain way that they stand or how they walk, and you be like, 'Man, I bet that pussy fire!'"

Kayla looked at him with a raised eyebrow. "No. You're weird."

Omar muffed her face. "Shut up, nigga."

Kayla narrowed her eyes at him. "Keep fuckin' with me, and the next time I braid ya hair, ya might develop a bald spot somewhere."

"I wish you would," he dared.

Kayla laughed her ass off.

"What did you do to ol' girl anyways?" she asked him right as Smoke and Haze started licking her face.

"Dragged her ass to the curb. It's garbage day. Smoke bit her booty too. Almost ripped her cheek off."

Just then, they both heard a loud crash come from outside. Omar hopped up and ran to the window. Kayla limped behind him, the Percocet already kicking in, taking the pain away.

Down by the curb, they both saw a half-naked Yajaira kicking and throwing the garbage cans at the tip of the driveway around, screaming and cursing Omar out, while holding her sore ass cheek.

"Trashy ass bitch," Omar muttered.

"Garbage ass ho," Kayla added.

They both burst out laughing then.

***

Damn! That ass is phat! And she bad than a muhfucka too! thought Jason as he laid eyes on the thick ass, chocolate chick that pulled up on the clean Kawasaki Ninja.

He loved him a dark-skinned chick with a fat ass. The leather leggings she had on shined like they were patent leather. She wore leather riding boots and a small, tight-fitting shirt with a low cleavage line that revealed ample breasts. When she took her helmet off, he saw long, luscious hair that was the color of rust fall down her back like a river of red wine.

Holy shit! A red head too! I'm on it! he told himself and immediately left the gas pump nozzle in the spout of his Infiniti truck's gas tank.

Jason went right up to the stunning biker chick, as she leaned her crotch-rocket on its kickstand.

"Excuse me, gorgeous," he spoke, stopping a few feet away. "I don't mean to disturb you, but yo, real rap, I have never seen such a beautiful woman hop off a bike until you did."

She smiled at him. "Is that so?"

"Yes. I have no need to cap. I'm Jason. It's nice to meet you. What's your name, if you don't mind me askin'?"

"My friends call me HaHa," she said.

Jason's brows furrowed. "HaHa? Like laughing?"

She nodded. "They say I'm funny, so it kind of just stuck."

Jason laughed.

"See?" the girl said with a chuckle.

"Damn. Beautiful and funny and I don't see a ring on ya finger."

"Not married and not in a relationship. I haven't met a single guy that can handle a bitch like me."

"Hmmm... I could show you that you just been in the presence of the wrong ones if you lemme get ya number."

She looked at him for a second. He peeped her eyes go down, likely checking out his swag, then back up to meet his eyes. A flirtatious smile then grew, making him gaze at her juicy lips.

"Where's ya phone?" she asked, licking her lips.

***

"Yessiir!" Jason shouted, as he started his engine. "Bagged a bad ass bitch! Lil mama gon' be ridin' this dick on the first night, yo! Watch!"

29

Jason pulled off and exited the gas station. He got his iPhone out and made a call, as he headed toward Garfield from Homewood.

"Nigga, where the fuck you at wit' that money, yo?" Tuck demanded to know.

"Chill, bro. I was getting gas. I'm ridin' up Hamilton right now 'bout to pass Fifth Ave. I'm comin', cutty."

"Hurry the fuck up! I gotta take a trip, and I need the rest of the cake!"

Tuck ended the call without another word.

"Angry ass nigga. Get some pussy or somethin', yo," Jason said, turning up the music.

Wiz Khalifa's *Tweak is Heavy* was on. It bumped from the twelve-inch subs in the rear. Nodding his head, Jason rapped along with the Taylor Gang creator.

Coming to a red light at Hamilton and East Liberty Boulevard where a big post office was, Jason was just about to make a right turn when the chick on the crotch-rocket pulled up in the left turn lane next to him. Jason turned his music down and rolled down his window, smiling at her.

"You followin' me now, gorgeous?" he asked, speaking loud, so she could hear him with her helmet on.

Suddenly, Jason felt a wire wrap around his neck from behind him. He immediately grabbed at it, trying to yank it off him. The hands that were pulling it were strong. The wire dug into his neck. He choked, struggling to breathe. Jason put up a fight, but fifteen seconds later, he took his last breath.

∗∗∗

Jerrica flipped the visor to her helmet up, as Chante got out of the Infiniti truck.

"Haha, bitch nigga!" she laughed, pointing at the dead money transporter. "Dumbass nigga thought he had a bitch goin'."

Chante hurried and got the bookbags of cash from the rear next to the big JL Audio speakers, then she jumped onto the back of the Ninja. Before Jerrica rode off, she pulled out a small black cylindrical device from her hoodie pocket, pulled the pin out of the top, and tossed it in through the driver's window. She kicked it into gear and dipped off seconds before the incendiary grenade blew the SUV up, destroying any trace of evidence that Chante had been inside.

Chapter 3

The following afternoon, Kayla woke up, groaning as the pain in her leg pounded. Even with the sunlight shining in through the floor-to-ceiling window of the magnificent guest bedroom Omar laid her in, she was still feeling glum and downtrodden. Shay's face popped into her head. Tears welled up in her eyes, as that crazy ass night rewound inside of her head.

I swear, Shay. I'ma get that nigga for you, cuz. On me, yo, Kayla mentally spoke, hoping Shay could hear.

After she took a few breaths, she noticed a bunch of boxes and bags with designer labels on them. Carefully, she swung herself around and crawled from under the covers in one of Omar's shirts. Making her way toward the end of the bed, she couldn't help but to smile at Omar's gracious gesture.

"My nigga, yo," she said to herself, appreciating her homie for the gifts.

Kayla carefully stood up. Pain hit her like a jolt of electricity. She grabbed her bottle of Percs off the nightstand, popped two, and mashed them down. Limping over to where a brand-new iPhone was, she laid eyes on a flat wooden box painted black with Cabot Guns engraved on it.

She opened it and gasped when she saw two custom 1911 .45 caliber semi-autos inside made completely of Damascus steel. Kayla was wowed by how they looked. They were like looking at how engine oil made swirls and other crazy shapes when it came in contact with water. She had never seen such beautiful guns in her life.

"Daaaamn, yo! Homiez, these muhfuckas is hard, yo!" she exclaimed, picking the two nearly $40,000 pistols up and holding them in her hands. "These muhfuckas are so clean! I can't wait to get 'em dirty!" she told herself, getting back on the bed.

"I bet you can't."

Kayla shrieked, startled by Omar's sudden appearance. She turned and saw him leaned against the doorway frame, shirtless, wearing Nike basketball shorts, Air Jordan 12s, and workout gloves over his hands. Smoke and Haze were at his side as well.

His muscular, tatted body was bulging from his strenuous workout. Kayla felt a hot wave shoot through her. Her eyes feasted on the 6'0" tall goon. The sight of her GQ handsome childhood friend had her felling shy as hell all of a sudden.

Omar stepped into the room. Kayla grew nervous as hell, as he got closer to her. Even though she had a bra and panties on under his shirt, he made her feel like she was naked and way too damn excited to see him.

Coming to a stop at her side, Kayla got a whiff of sweat and manly musk. It started making her want to bite him and lick him. Smoke and Haze hopped up onto the bed and laid at her sides to help comfort her.

"How you feel, girlrilla?" Omar asked her.

"Well, I just popped a couple of pills, so soon, I'll be aight," she told him, trying so hard not to stare at his unreal six-pack abs.

"Yo, don't be getting addicted to them Percs, Kay. I'll really put my foot up ya ass if you do."

"Nigga, I don't get addicted to shit but gun smoke and gettin' money! Fuck you mean, yo?"

Omar laughed. "Now that's my girlrilla! Talk that gangsta shit, Ma!"

Kayla burst out laughing, as she stroked behind the dogs' ears.

"Y'all's pappy is crazy, Smoke and Haze."

"Come on. Let's get you in the shower and change ya bandages. We can eat, then I got a move to make, and you are comin' wit' me. Non-negotiable."

Omar kissed her on the forehead and left out. Smoke and Haze licked her face then followed him out. Kayla sighed to herself. Smiling, a very vivid fantasy popped into her head that immediately made her nipples grow hard.

"No. Uh uh. Not happenin'," she told herself. "That nigga is a thot, and he ain't even good lookin'."

Kayla paused and closed her eyes, shaking her head at herself, knowing damn well she just told a big, dumbass lie to herself.

***

After she showered, Omar helped her dress her wounds and put new bandages on them then wrapped them up. She then pulled out a custom-made outfit that Omar had designed exclusively for her. The tight-fitting jacket and pants sweatsuit was like a Fabletics workout set. It was blue with Girlrilla in silver letters all over the jacket and the leggings with a silver tank top to go with it. On her feet, she put on the new blue, white, and silver Retro Jordan 4s that he got her, threw her long locs into a ponytail, then checked herself in the mirror. Smiling at herself, she grabbed her new iPhone and limped out of the room to go meet up with Omar.

Down in the big grand foyer, Kayla saw Omar in an Amir fit with the bone jacket and bone sneakers and a Richard Mille RM 16-02 Extra-flat on his wrist, and his braids were messy yet alluring to her. Kayla again found herself entranced with Omar so much that she just could not stop staring at him. She was seeing something in him now that she hadn't noticed before, and she found herself desiring to know exactly what it was.

"You good?" Omar asked her.

"Yes. Thanks for the fit. It's dope, O," Kayla told him.

He nodded. "No doubt. Let's be out," he told her then whistled for his dogs.

Oh, my God... Kayla got ass! Goddammit! That muhfucka so fat! Aw, shit! O, man, fuck is wrong wit'chu, nigga? That's ya homegirl, and she just lost her cousin tryna collect some money for you! Pig ass nigaaa! Goddamn that ass is fat!

Omar battled his own thoughts, as he tried to keep his eyes off of forty-six-inches of jiggly booty in tight ass leggings, but the flesh was weak, and he was yearning to squeeze on it and smack on it.

Out in the six-car garage, Omar hit his wireless key fob remote and opened the third bay door. The door rolled up, and his exclusive, new, Blu Corsa, blue 2024 Ferrari Purosangue truck was revealed, sitting on blue-painted twenty-three-inch Forgiato rims that allowed the yellow brake calipers to show.

"Oh, snap! My nigga got the 'Rari truck!" Kayla beamed, wide-eyed with shock, as she looked at the $750,000, four-door exotic SUV.

"Yeah. Had to. I gotta stay ahead of them other clown ass niggas," Omar replied, walking her to the passenger door. "You gon' be pushin' one of these joints soon too, yo."

He opened the door for her and the rear for the dogs. Helping Kayla up inside the white and blue accented interior, Omar closed the door, then he got up behind the wheel. Kayla got goosebumps when the big, twin-turbo, V12 engine started up. Cheesing her ass off, she reached over to the stereo and put on some tunes, as Omar pulled out of the garage. She turned it up when she heard GloRilla's *Phat Nall*. Leaning back in her seat, she got ready to go wherever Omar was taking her. As long as she was with him, she ain't give a damn where it was.

Leaving out of Plum, Omar made a stop at McDonald's for food then got to the Edgewood-Swissvale area. He hopped off the parkway and made his way up Rankin.

Minutes later, he turned into a business owned by his homie that was dubbed Crip Towin', LLC.

A long garage with multiple bays was to the left. A row of custom painted and chromed out foreigns were lined up next to each other. Omar pulled up and parked next to a black wicked looking Ford F-150 Shelby Super Snake pickup truck sitting low to the ground on big rims. He cut the engine and got out, letting his dogs out, then went around to help Kayla out.

Coming out of the office was Ace, a tall, lanky, light brown-skinned guy with a razor-sharp hairline, beard, and messy, Rasta style dreads. He had on a work shirt with Ace Customs on it, Dickies, and Timberlands. He immediately rushed up to Kayla and hugged her emphatically, beyond happy to see her.

"Yooo, lil sis! Man, I'm glad you aight, yo! I'm sorry about Shay. On Crip, my nigga, that nigga, Tuck, gon' lay down real soon!"

Nodding with appreciation, Kayla refrained from informing him that action was already being taken by her girlrilla gang. She hadn't even told Omar. They would find out, real soon, how crazy her girls were.

"Thanks, bro. I know you gon' bring it to that bitch ass nigga. Make him beg for his life when you do," Kayla told him with an innocent smile.

Ace nodded his head. Looking at Omar, he told him that he put fifty bricks in the Shelby pickup's trap along with a Draco and a couple of back-up Glocks.

"Y'all need me to ride?" he then asked.

"Naw, we good, yo. It's there, spend a day or so out there, then back wit' the money. Easy like before. Plus, I got the girlrilla and my killas wit' me," Omar told him. "Keep ya ears open and eyes on Tuck. I'ma be plannin' Shay's funeral. After we honor her, we murder him."

"Yup. I holla'd at Kurt too, bro. He was happy to let niggaz know that the last two investments we made have been earnin' real good."

"Cool. I'll get at him soon," Omar assured him then received the keys to the Shelby truck and dapped Ace up.

He assisted Kayla up into the sleek black and silver leather interior, while the dogs got in back. Behind the wheel, he started up the insanely powerful supercharged V8 engine. 775 horses shook the pickup, ready to get to galloping along the highway. Kayla got goosebumps from the sound of pure power.

"You ready, girlrilla?" Omar asked, looking over at her, giving her that million-dollar smile that made her feel like a hot fudge sundae on a hot day, ready to be licked and slurped by a tongue that craved sweetness.

"Yessir, my nigga. To wherever we goin' and beyond!" she replied excitedly. Then, as Omar pulled off, she reached over to the music, then turned it on, and found a playlist of Ridin' Tunes, selecting it to play.

Rich Gangsta by King Von and Tee Grizzley started playing. Kayla reclined her chair and relaxed, happy to be rolling with Omar on a money mission, like a girlrilla was supposed to do with her nigga.

***

Pissed as shit, Tuck sat in the backroom of his little convenience store on Frankstown Avenue, close to Wheeler Street in Homewood. The news of his money being taken had him so hot that he could breathe fire. He knew it was Omar's retaliation. He hadn't expected him to hit back that fast because he knew the guy, Omar, never retaliated right away. He let his opps think he wasn't coming, then when he did strike, it was catastrophic.

It was only a one hundred-thousand-dollar loss, but still, Tuck didn't want to lose a dime, especially because niggaz put pussy above staying focused on getting money. Shaking his head at Jason's stupidity, he sat up and grabbed the half-smoked blunt of exotic from the ashtray. He flamed up, puffing on it, and his eyes rolled over to the big, seventy-two-inch HDTV mounted on the wall. The news was on. He smirked at it when he saw the reporter was outside of the spot he and his homies hit up and relieved Omar of just over three hundred and fifty thousand in cash, dope, and some guns. The faces of the four dudes and the chick he and his goons left to burn came on the screen, labeled victims. He started laughing then.

"Aye, yo, Tuck?"

Tuck looked at the doorway and saw his huge bone-crusher there.

"What's up, Escalade?" Tuck asked before taking another puff of the exotic.

"Ya college squad's here, and they brought some random ass bitch. That say she need to get at you."

He furrowed his eyebrows, then turning his head to the right, he looked at the security camera monitor screen. He saw nineteen-year-old Whiz, his twenty-two-year-old sister, Nala, and a deep dark chocolate chick in a white, short-sleeved top, tight, denim, skinny leg jeans, with white, stiletto pumps on her feet, and her hair up in a bun on her head.

"Bring 'em in," Tuck ordered and stubbed the blunt out.

Escalade left out. He returned a minute later with the light-skinned, Lacoste Polo-clad Whiz, who was skinny and sported a fresh, old school style, high top, bald fade, his voluptuous coffee-brown sister, clad in a neon-green Chanel shoulder-less mini dress that fit her like a second skin with monogrammed pink double 'C's all over it that matched her long hair, her diamond-stitched handbag, the Chanel watch on her wrist, and the pointed-toe six-inch pumps on her feet.

Tuck's eyes ogled Nala with lust. Her pink glossy lips had his dick hardening up, as he replayed the last time they were wrapped around his dick. Then, he looked at the stallion that was with them. She was stupid thick. Tuck felt like he was looking at a broke version of Megan Thee Stallion, as his eyes roamed all over her. Escalade left the three with him and closed the door. Tuck looked at Whiz and Nala.

"Who is this?" he asked them, looking at the beautiful woman.

"The answer to ya problems," the chick told him before either of the two could speak.

"This was Omar's bitch," Whiz then said, stifling a laugh.

Nala snickered to herself as well, finding it hilarious what the chick had told them when she was going off about getting back at Omar for doing her dirty and letting his dog bite her in the ass. They had been at one of their people's cribs in Wilkinsburg when she came in pissed and talking big shit. The girl was a friend of their friend, and once she got to spitting Omar's name, Whiz and Nala offered her a hand in getting revenge right away.

"Oh, word?" Tuck looked at her. "What's ya name?"

"Yajaira. I need you to put that nigga in the ground for me, Tuck! Real rap, yo! His ass need to go!"

"You two, out. But stay close," Tuck told Whiz and Nala.

"Fuck you mean out, nigga?" Nala shot back, putting her hands on her hips and scowling at him.

"O-U-T! Out! Bye!" Tuck yelled.

Whiz laughed, while his sister smacked her lips. They left out and closed the door, leaving Yajaira with Tuck.

"So, you want Omar dead, huh? Why you came to me? Why not just feed his ass food wit' poison in it? Or pop his ass while he sleep?"

"Because a bitch like me needs taken care of. If I did that without lockin' down another nigga wit' cake that's better than his bitch ass, then I'ma be bummin' it on the streets."

Tuck was surprised by her honesty but turned off by that gold digger shit. Nevertheless, he knew exactly what to do with a devious bitch like her.

"Plus," Yajaira continued, making her way toward him, strutting like a model, swaying her wide hips with a starry-eyed look on her face, "I know a few girls that used to fuck wit'chu'. They say that you got that bomb-ass dick. A bitch need that as much as I need bank rolls in my bag."

Tuck started grinning at her. He looked at her juicy lips and visualized them wrapped around his length.

"I hear you talkin' bout what you need, but what I need," he spoke, undoing the button and zipper on his 501s, "is for you to drop down and show me how that neck feels right now."

She licked her lips, as he pulled out his thick eleven-inch anaconda. Looking up at the dark-brown skinned man's face, his 6'2" tall frame dwarfed her by nine inches. Without a word, Yajaira sank down to her knees, wrapped her left hand around the base of his cock, and opened her mouth, sticking her tongue out.

Tuck stared down at her, as she licked all around the tip of his dick then licked her way down to his nuts. She took them into her mouth and sucked on them, jerking his cock at the same time.

"Goddamn! Shit!" Tuck groaned, loving it.

She spit his balls out a minute later. Opening her mouth wide, she engulfed his monstrous dick and tried to swallow all of him. She gagged on it when eight inches reached the back of her throat.

Tuck grabbed her head and started fucking her face ruthlessly. He cursed, groaning, as he went nuts on her. He felt her hand cup his balls and massage them. About a minute later, he felt his nut rising. He let her head go and let her take over.

She gripped his length with both hands and jerked, while she sucked, taking him the rest of the way. He groaned gutturally, as his nut came. Pulling his dick out of her mouth, he told her to open wide. She stuck her tongue out and all too willingly let him cum all over her face. She moaned as globs of hot sperm splattered on her mug, trickling downwards toward her mouth. She licked up what she could, then she kissed the tip of his dick, looking up at him with mischievous eyes.

"Okay, then, Yajaira," Tuck spoke, definitely digging the shameless freak's aim to please. "I'ma need to know everything you know about that nigga, Omar. Where he lives, where all his spots are, everything."

"Oh, I can do that, baby," she agreed, getting up off of her knees with cum still all over her face, "but can a bitch get somethin' to wipe this shit up off my mug?"

Before Tuck could answer her, an explosion from outside the office shook the whole store building, then machine gunfire erupted.

"What the fuck?" Tuck ran back to his desk and grabbed his Desert Eagle .40 from the drawer.

Yajaira started panicking. "What the hell goin' on?"

"You tell me! You tryna set a nigga up, bitch?" he demanded to know, glaring at her, while it sounded like a warzone outside of his door.

"No!" Yajaira snapped.

The door flew open just then. Tuck pointed his cannon toward it, seconds away from dumping, when he saw it was Whiz and Nala, both of them with Glocks in their hands.

"We gotta go! *Now!*" Whiz shouted, running toward the rear emergency exit in Tuck's office.

Tuck then saw Escalade run in, carrying a Mossberg pump. He slammed the door shut and turned to run when bullets flew through the door, slamming into his back and the back of his head. The massive man fell face forward, dead before he hit the floor.

"Tuck! Come on!" Nala shouted.

Snapped out of his trance, Tuck ran toward the rear exit where Whiz and Nala anxiously waited.

"Wait for me!" he heard Yajaira shout.

Tuck turned around and saw her running in his direction, looking petrified. He raised his DE up and pointed it right at her face before she made it to him. She screamed, slipping, as she tried to jump out of the line of fire. Right as she landed on her ass, the main door to his office exploded and in ran three figures in black hooded sweatsuits with some serious fire power in their hands.

***

Chante, Jerrica, and Valerie immediately saw Tuck, the young dude, and the bitch in the bright green Chanel dress that had hopped out of the Range Rover with the thick chick in the white shirt and tight jeans. The girl was on her ass when they ran in after Chante blew the door to pieces with the grenade-launcher attachment on her AR-15.

Locking eyes with Tuck, she and her girlrillas took aim to fire, but so did the young guy and the girl, while Tuck ran out of the back door.

Brrrrrrrr!

Brrrrrrrrr!

Brrrrrrrrrr!

They started dumping before the two youngsters could. They dipped out of the door, narrowly missing the storm of slugs flying at them by mere inches.

"*Fuck!*" Chante cursed.

She ran after them, hellbent on catching Tuck and murking him for what he did to Shay.

Jerrica and Valerie followed, bypassing the chick. They got outside to see Tuck's Scat Pack Dodge Challenger speeding down the brick-paved alley toward Wheeler. Chante fired a grenade at the rear of it but missed when it reached Wheeler and bent the corner. The grenade hit the building across the street and blew a huge hole in it.

"Motherfucker!" she screamed angrily.

A noise behind them made them all turn back toward the back of the store. They saw the dark-skinned chick hurrying out, as the fire inside rapidly spread.

"Thank God y'all came! That bitch ass nigga was gon' kill me! Yo, y'all need to let me roll wit' y'all. I can help y'all get his ass! He after this big dog named Omar, and I'm Omar's chick!"

Chante raised up an eyebrow. "You're Yajaira?"

The girl's brows furrowed. "Uh… yeah. Do I know you?"

"Naw. But Kayla does, and she does not like you. Seein' that she is my homie, you gots to go. Buh-bye!"

"No! Wait!" Yajaira screamed, but her pleas fell upon deaf ears, as Chante took aim at her and fired a grenade at her.

Yajaira's entire body exploded. Blood, guts, and bone fragments splattered all over the alleyway, making it look like a bloody mess. Chante, Jerrica, and Valerie took off up the alley, hurrying to get back to where Valerie had parked the late 80's model Jeep she had stolen that was parked up on Frankstown by an age's old music store across from a big park and get up out of there before the area was swarmed by Pittsburgh police cars.

Chapter 4

Kayla cursed as she read the text that had just came to her iPhone.

The chicken had flown the coop. No wings tonight but bye-bye to O's shmutt bucket.

Happy to hear Yajaira was out of there for good but pissed that Tuck had not been laid down too, Kayla blanked out of her phone. She heard Omar on the phone, as she put hers back on the charger.

"Why am I not surprised?" she heard him ask with a chuckle, then he ended the call. "I'm guessin' that was the work of the girlrilla gang down at Tuck's little candy store, huh?"

Kayla shook her head and leaned back.

"He killed my cousin and shot me. Homiez, niggaz is not getting away wit' that. Ya' lil bitch got her ass spanked too."

Omar's eyebrows furrowed. "Who?"

"Yajaira, nigga! Man, you a thot, O! Homiez, you are!"

He couldn't help but laugh at that. "Don't be mad 'cause bitches love me, Kay."

"Whatever, nigga! Fuck them hoes! I want Tuck! Dead!"

"Me too, Kay. But we gotta remember to move smart and keep his ass creepin' on eggshells. He gets real cocky. Let that clown ass nigga fuck his own shit up. Then we get him. Period. Aight?"

"Sure, Omar. Whatever you say," Kayla replied then tuned him out for the remainder of the ride.

***

44

Do it! Hit everything! He gots to go! I know it was O that sent them at me! Do your job and lay down the law!

"Guess we got work to do, Cammie," said Amber, reading the text from Tuck. "Our dumbass benefactor has requested our services again."

Cammie wiped the sweet powder from her donut from her puffed up lips then took a sip of her coffee.

"Lemme guess... Omar?"

"Yep. Never ends. Since Tuck was released, he's been trying to win what used to be his back. It's a shame that nobody knows how to move on."

"Well, who give a shit? If he wants to keep on payin' us to do his dirty work, then I have no problem bein' his dirt devil," Cammie replied. "Make sure he sends payment before we move. Not going through that bullshit again with his 'I got you later' ass."

Amber sent the reply for their upfront fee to be issued before they got up then set her phone down. She picked her own donut back up and took a bite, loving the delicious homemade pastry's fruit filling and glazed outside that Homewood's famed Dana's made so well and had been since before Amber and her partner were even born just over thirty years ago.

On her second bite, Amber's iPhone dinged. She saw a wire transfer deposited into the 'business' account in the amount of $25,000.

"We have a down payment, girl," she told Cammie, showing her the notification.

Cammie nodded. "Alright then. Let's finish these delicious donuts then we can go," she replied then picked up a glazed long-john with cinnamon apple filling and took a bite. "Mmm! This is like sex! Woo!"

Amber laughed as she picked up her next pastry, a glazed cinnamon roll topped with maple icing, and took a bite, plotting on getting the job done while remaining as lowkey

CHRISTOPHER "DIESEL" HORNEZES

as she and her partner in crime had been for the last ten years that they had been for hire.

***

Just under eight hours later, Kayla, behind the wheel, giving Omar a break, crossed into Illinois from Indiana. Following directions, she stayed on I-90/I-94 North, shooting through Chicago Skyway Toll Booth then half an hour later, Chicago. Passing through the big city on the Dan Ryan was new to her. Kayla had only been outside of PA to New Jersey, New York, Ohio, Michigan, Virginia, West Virginia, Maryland, and D.C. Being in a city that was well-known for being the hub of everything sellable for the entire Midwest was different, intriguing even, with multi-billion-dollar commerce chains, trillions of dollars' worth of imported and exported goods moving all around, to gangs, guns, dope, corruption, and the treachery in the streets and in the police.

Continuing north, breaking off the E-Way, she hopped on the Edens, taking it up to Highland Park, where she was told to stay left as I-94 branched off from the start of Illinois Route 41. Taking 41 North, she passed through a number of suburban towns until she came up to a big four-way up in Zion where 41 intersected with Route 173.

To avoid the commercial truck weight station ahead, where Illinois State Troopers posted and loved pulling over nice vehicles, just to see who was driving, Omar had Kayla get off the highway and take 173 East farther into Zion. Ten minutes later, she came to Green Bay Road. He had her go left, then she took Green Bay into Wisconsin, entering Kenosha just over fifteen minutes later.

Coming to Green Bay and Highway 50, he told her they were going to the big shopping plaza to their left. Kayla made her way into the city-block long plaza, going around the back way where trucks brought in cargo to all the stores.

At the rear of a furniture store, he told her to back up to where a tall garage door was. She did and came to a stop just a few feet away from it.

Omar sent a quick text and waited a minute. The tall door began rising seconds later. Inside was lit up brightly from lights all around. Kayla backed the Shelby pickup inside the loading/unloading part and killed the engine.

The door slowly closed back down. Omar opened his door to get out. Kayla's peripheral caught sight of a door to her left opening. A woman stepped out, a very glamorous woman. She had long, lustrous, dirty blonde hair that was curled in perfect spirals. Her face was model-like with high cheekbones, exotic blue eyes, a little nose, and glossy, perky lips. Kayla guessed that in the red-wine colored pointed-toe Red Bottoms she had on, she was an inch taller than what she stood.

The woman had an olive skin tone and was amazingly stacked with wide hips, big tits, and a fat ass. She was dressed classy yet dick-teasing sexy in a yellow Louis Vuitton blouse with ruffled sleeves and a low-cleavage line, a red-wine, leather, Louis Vuitton flared mini-skirt, nude pantyhose with diamond patterns, and diamond encrusted, yellow-gold jewelry. Kayla could tell that the lady was not an ordinary furniture store owner.

"Oooomaaaarrr!" the chick sang out excitedly when he got out of the truck.

She ran to him, throwing herself in his arms, wrapping her arm around him and squeezing him. "Oh, my God, baby, I am so frickin' happy your ass is here!"

Baby? Kayla mentally questioned, hearing what the girl had just called him.

In the backseat, Smoke grunted then nudged Kayla's elbow with his nose. Haze sneezed then barked at her. Omar walked around the front end of the truck and opened Kayla's door.

"Kay, this is my partner, Claudia," he introduced. "Claudia, this my best friend, Kayla."

Claudia was even more beautiful close up. Her smile was very cheerful and warming. Kayla found the woman's aura to be refreshing.

"Nice to meet you, Kayla. Heard a lot about you."

"Have you now?" Kayla looked at Omar with a raised eyebrow. "All good things I would hope."

"Definitely," Claudia replied, as Omar grinned goofily. "He speaks very highly of you, like a baby sister type of way."

Baby sister, my ass! Kayla thought, creeped out that he could see her as that when she knew that he was attracted to her.

"Soooo!" Omar interrupted, taking Kayla's hand and helping her out. "How about we get to the bizness and chat a little later?"

"Sounds good to me, handsome," Claudia agreed, all the while giving Omar a look that made Kayla want to smack her dumb.

Standing to the side with Smoke and Haze, Kayla watched Omar reach under the side of the pickup's bed and hit a button. The secret compartment that was fabricated by Ace unlocked. He flipped the side of the bed up and revealed fifty kilos strapped in tightly.

Claudia rolled a little cart over to him. He removed thirty kilos of cocaine first, all marked with blue tape, then he removed the remaining twenty, all of them stuffed with raw heroin marked with gold tape. Closing the trap, Omar told Kayla to follow. Smoke and Haze trotted alongside her. They all followed Claudia through a door into a brightly lit hallway. She wheeled the cart into a door on her left, holding the door open for them to enter.

The room was filled with furniture, wrapped in plastic, some with signs that said 'sold', others with 'reserved'.

"The two purple couches, O," Claudia told him, as she wheeled the dope to where a large area carpet covered the middle of the floor.

Kayla went with Omar to the couches. He opened one up like a futon. Stashed inside were stacks of big faces, all in shrink-wrapped plastic. The cushions were filled with cash, the arm rests, the footrests that kicked up when the recline lever was pulled back, and the backrest. The second couch was filled with cash as well. Omar smiled at the beautiful sight.

"Two and a half mil' split between the two, baby," Claudia informed him.

Kayla saw that she had flipped the rug over. A hidden safe in the floor was being opened.

"Sounds like one hell of a Christmas is comin'," Omar chuckled, as Claudia began stashing the dope. "Everything been aight out here though?"

"For the most part. Dude's bitch ass keeps trying to get me to let him back into mine and Valentino's life."

"Heeeell no! You better not, Claudia! Homiez, I'll put that bitch ass nigga to sleep if he comes anywhere near y'all again!"

Kayla furrowed her brows, lost as to whom they were speaking of. She asked no questions though. She was sure Omar would fill her in if there was a need.

"Relax, baby. My baby daddy is a loser and a fucking peon. He ain't forget that ass whoopin' you put on him the last time he called himself comin' to my spot and getting stupid."

Seeing Omar's nostrils flare, Kayla knew that whoever this baby daddy was, Omar despised him. How he was still alive, Kayla was stumped.

"Fuck that bitch ass nigga, yo! Homiez, he a bitch! Pure bitch!" Omar seethed.

Well damn! This nigga is really mad! Over her though? Kayla wondered, curious about how Omar and Claudia even knew each other.

Claudia put the last kilo in her safe. She closed it, put the rug back over it, then looked at Omar. Walking up to him, she put her arms around him, pressing herself up against him.

Aw, hell naw! This nigga fuckin' her too? Kayla's eyes remained glued on the two. Watching Claudia put her lips to Omar's made her almost vomit. She then leaned in and whispered something in Omar's ear.

Claudia looked at Kayla then.

"I need to talk to Omar about some business really quick. I'll bring him right back, okay?"

"Uh huh," Kayla replied dryly, rolling her eyes.

Claudia giggled then took Omar's hand, escorting him out of the storage room to God knows where.

Kayla looked at Smoke and Haze. They sat at her side, panting, tongues out, looking up at her.

"I don't know about y'all, but I'm hungry. How bout we leave ya shmutt ass father here for a lil' bit wit' his big booty… whatever she is and go get some food?"

Smoke stood up and barked, tail wagging eagerly. Haze stood, ears perked up, knowing and loving the word food.

"Let's go then," Kayla told them then led the way back to the garage.

She let them up into the pickup, climbed behind the wheel first, then realized she had to open the garage. She went to the button on the wall and pushed it. The door started rolling up. She pulled the pickup out of the garage, got out to close the door, then got back in.

"Okay, monsters. Let's go see what's still open at this time of night."

***

"Aye! Look! The door! It's rollin' up, fam!" Sneaky excitedly squeaked to his guys that he was in the stolen Trackhawk with.

Behind the wheel, J Wop saw a black-on-black pickup truck exiting the furniture store's rear garage port. The other two in the Jeep, Wonnie and Lil Moe, all got geeked up when they saw the pickup pull out. They had been sitting in the parking lot of a townhouse, parked across from the rear of the shopping plaza, for an hour. They had seen it pull up and back inside then the door closed.

The four youngsters were part of a clique that was well-known around Kenosha. They were called the EBK Boys, and to them, anyone could get it if they weren't EBK. One of their O.G.s put them on the lick. He told them that the owner of the furniture store moved big kilos of coke and dope, but nobody would ever guess by the way she dressed and acted.

The EBK Boys knew the man's reputation rang bells in the K. He was a monster in the streets and all about that mighty dollar. If he said it, it was law. So, they put a plan together, snatched a fast whip, strapped up, and went to post up and wait for their chance, which looked like it had come.

"Come on, nigga! Let's go! Follow it, fam," Sneaky urged, pulling out his Glock equipped with a switch and a fifty-round drum.

The others had the same type of guns with extra drums. They had prepared heavily. The amount of money the O.G. said left out of there, they knew they had to be ready. No fuck ups and no survivors.

J Wop started the engine, put it in drive, and pulled out of the parking spot he was in. He got on the pickup truck's trail but stayed back so as to not spook the driver.

"Eeeee, joe, we bout to get this money! Yo, get ready!" Sneaky told his guys. "On EBK, we get the gwop and kill the driver! Period!"

Chapter 5

"Ohh! Oooohh! Omar! Oh, God, oh, God, oh, Gooood! Yes! Ohh, fuck! Shit, baby!" Claudia cried out with bliss, as Omar worked his pussy eating magic on her. She sat up on the top of her desk, blouse off, bra gone, allowing succulent 36 DD cups to be free. Omar had her skirt up around her waist, pantyhose and panties at her ankles, her pumps still on, legs up, and his face buried between her thick thighs. Claudia leaned back, using her hands to balance herself, while he slurped and sucked on her clit. Her head spun around in circles, her body trembling, his lips and tongue taking her places that hardly any other man had managed to take her to ever before.

Omar had wanted to resist her; Kayla was there with him, but Omar never could resist her. Claudia was bad – thick as hell, a go-getter by definition, and a fucking freak! He remembered when he first met her down at a dog show in Atlanta, one that was dedicated to personal protection/guard/attack dogs. He had gone there when Smoke and Haze were pups, hoping to gain first-hand knowledge from people in that industry. He met Claudia, who had been doing the same for her two Blue Blood Cane Corso pups. The attraction between each other was instantaneous. Claudia adored men of color, and while Omar loved all women of all races, when he saw how much of a distinctive Mediterranean-type look she had and discovered that she was full-blooded Albanian, he had to get her naked and sweaty.

And he did, over and over and over again, nearly getting caught up by the father of her young son once in a hotel down in Chicago. Omar then learned how much of a punk ass, bitch ass shmuck Claudia's baby daddy was and how jealous of her success thus far he was, and it made Omar want to bury the bitch ass nigga alive. But for the sake of Claudia's two-year old son, who she had when she was thirty, Omar let the guy breathe... for the moment.

"Omar! Oh, God! I'm gonna cum, baby!" Claudia cried, feeling it coming on strong.

He slid two fingers in between her slick pussy lips and finger fucked her while sucking her clit. Claudia screamed out his name, as the blissful sensation increased tenfold, causing her to erupt like never before. She exploded, cumming so hard that she squirted in his face.

"Shit!" Claudia cursed then took deep breaths to try and fill her lungs with air.

Omar stood, face wet, dick throbbing. He dropped his Amiri jeans and boxer briefs, ready to beat the pussy up, until Claudia stopped him.

"My turn, big Daddy," she told him then slid off the desk, dropping to her knees before him.

Omar, with absolute glee, watched as she puckered her plumped red lips and kissed the bulbous tip of his dick, while her hand was wrapped around the base of his manhood. She ran her tongue down the side, stopping at his balls. She kissed them then licked them, slathering them with saliva. Omar shuddered at the tingly sensation that her tongue was giving him. It made his toes curl up in his Amiri sneakers.

"Shit, Ma! Damn, that feel good!" he groaned out.

Claudia sucked his balls into her mouth and pleasured them. She could feel him shaking. The sounds of his groaning aroused her even more. Making him weak with her naturally freaky nature was something she lived for. It gave her more of a thrill than moving large amounts of coke and dope.

Claudia took his dick into her left hand and started jerking him, while his nuts were in her mouth. Omar cursed repeatedly, head thrown back, eyes squeezed shut. She was fucking his head up! She spit his balls out seconds later then engulfed nearly nine inches of him, taking him to the back of her throat. Omar's hands balled into fists. The pleasure was overwhelming. She had him ready to pop.

Claudia deep throated him then released him from her mouth. She spit a mixture of saliva and his pre cum back onto his cock, then after she slurped it back up, she inhaled him in again. Omar placed his hands on her head and started fucking her mouth, watching his dick go in and out, while her juicy red lips wrapped around him.

"Fuuuck!" he cursed again.

Claudia spit his dick out suddenly. She looked up at him with the naughtiest gaze ever. Standing up, she went to her desk, put her hands on it, and leaned over, letting all forty-five inches of Albanian ass fill his line of sight. Hypnotized by her full moon, Omar floated up behind her. He smacked her left cheek then took his cock into his hand. Claudia bent over all the way for him. He slid inside of her wetness, filling her up so perfectly that it made her lick her lips.

"Ohh, Omar! God, you feel so good!" Claudia moaned, as he started hitting it, gripping her hips, holding them tightly, jack hammering her so good that she couldn't stop crying out at the tops of her lungs.

***

What the fuck? thought Jerrod after he entered the furniture store using the security code he found at his baby mama's house.

Hearing loud moaning and cursing coming from the rear, he already knew that his nympho maniac baby mama was getting dicked down like he had nearly caught her red handed so many times with that light-skinned nigga with braids from out of town. Jerrod had been dying to catch dude up, but he continuously missed his opportunity. Not this time though.

Jerrod, black as charcoal and 6'4" of athletically built street nigga, had recently paroled out of a joint in Wisconsin. He came home with only a couple hundred dollars, no clothes, no shoes, no place to live, so he was staying in a TLP that Wisconsin's extended supervision agents placed him at until he got a place of his own.

His baby mama was good! She was rich! Dope girl rich and he was broke. When he got locked up for armed robbery, she immediately ghosted him. It bruised his ego in the worst way, and he vowed to get revenge when he came home.

After he broke into her house, luckily her dogs weren't there, Jerrod looked everywhere for her stash of cash that she normally kept in the floor safe under her bed. It wasn't in their son's room nor in her four-car garage. Pissed and ready to knock her shit back, Jerrod took the keys to her custom Jeep Wrangler Rubicon, fitted with a Hellcat engine, her big, bulky .44 Bulldog, and headed off to see if she was at the store. Sure enough, pulling into the massive parking lot where customer vehicles were steadily leaving out as the row of stores in the plaza reached closing time, Jerrod saw Claudia's blue Lamborghini Urus parked in front of her store. He parked a few rows away to wait until more people left. While he waited, knowing what day it was, Jerrod made a call as backup insurance so that no matter what, he got paid and the bitch lost her head...

Creeping through the store toward the sounds, Jerrod felt his pay-as-you-go phone vibrate in his pocket. He pulled it out and saw it was his young, hungry wolf.

"Yeah?" Jerrod answered.

"Aye, my nigga! We on it right now!" Sneaky told him. "This black pickup came up out the back of the store! We on its ass! Where you at, joe?"

"I'm handlin' business right now, fam. Just get that money and meet at the spot. Don't get stupid neither."

"Never that. See you in a few, joe."

Jerrod ended the call then. Tucking the phone back into his pocket, he started walking again. He got even closer. He heard his baby mama calling out some nigga's name like he was really fucking the shit out of her.

White hot jealousy filled Jerrod as he pushed through the double doors as quietly as he could. The moaning and screaming were coming from her office. Jerrod moved swiftly toward the door. When he reached it, he gently turned the knob. It was unlocked. He quietly opened the door just a crack, and peeking through, he saw Claudia getting fucked wildly from the back by some nigga with long braids rocking an Amiri fit.

The sight of the guy pounding his bitch like that had Jerrod seeing red. He reached his hand down into the waistline of his jeans and gripped the handle of the big Bulldog. Pulling it out, he thumbed the trigger back and got ready to interrupt the two… very rudely.

***

Gripped by tight walls of pleasure, swimming in a deep pool of ecstasy, Omar was trapped in his bliss, and he wasn't looking for a way out. He held onto her hips and jack hammered her until she reached her third climax, exploding all over his dick and thighs.

Omar pulled his joint out of the pussy. Grabbing her sweaty booty cheeks, he opened her up and spit down on her asshole. He rubbed the tip of his dick in it, lubing her up, so he could slide right in.

Claudia clenched her teeth, moaning, as she felt Omar's dick easing into her asshole. It went from pain to pleasure in mere seconds. His hands were on her hips again, holding her, while he worked her. She moaned his name, feeling it, loving it. She climaxed not even a minute later, drenching him once again.

Omar felt his nut rising soon after. He gritted his teeth and kept fucking her, but then, she yanked him out of her ass and was on her knees before him, mouth wide open, inviting him right in. He put his dick right back in her mouth and let her suck him until he bust his nut. He exploded in her mouth with a deep, guttural groan escaping him. Claudia wrapped her hands around his length and stroked, while she sucked all that was left out of him, filling her mouth all the way up.

Claudia opened her mouth, stuck her tongue out, and let his globs of sperm dribble down her chin, dripping onto her chest. Giggling at the starry-eyed gaze in his eyes from her triple X-rated grand finale, Claudia swallowed what wasn't on her chin or her chest, then she licked her lips clean of him.

"You seduced me... again," Omar said then chuckled about it.

He helped Claudia from the floor.

"And? You did say sex was just sex. Don't act like you haven't did the same to me, O."

"Not while someone was with you."

"Oh... yeah. Your friend. I guess we should get back to her before she thinks we left her."

"Kay knows I would never leave her, yo. Homiez, she's my ace."

Claudia made a noise that sounded like a grunt, as she pulled up her panties and her pantyhose. Omar fixed himself up as well.

"Hope she ain't mad. Come on. I need to get back to her," he said then made a beeline for the door.

Claudia let out an annoyed chuckle. She'd never seen Omar leave so fast after they fucked.

"She must be really special to him. His ass couldn't wait to get back to her."

Claudia followed him out of her office, back to the hallway that led to the storage room, but after three steps, she stopped and frowned. Omar stopped where he was and looked back at her. He saw the look on her face – bothered, suspicious.

"You aight?" he asked her.

Claudia looked at him. "I… don't know. It kind of feel like… like someone was… here."

"Like watching us?"

She shrugged.

Omar looked at her for a second then tried to see if he could sense what she did.

"Where's your dogs?" he asked her.

"With my son at the sitter's house. He hates it when they ain't with him."

Omar nodded. "Come on," he told her then turned to keep going. They got to the storage area. Kayla wasn't there, nor were the dogs.

"Yo, Kayla? You in here?" he called out.

No answer. Everything was as it was when he left.

Maybe she went back to the garage, Claudia thought.

Omar quickly stepped to the garage. The pickup was gone. Smoke and Haze were too.

"Maaan, where the hell did she go?"

Omar pulled his phone out and called her.

"What up?" she answered.

"Kay, where the hell you go, yo?"

"To get food, nigga. Me and the monsters was hungry."

"You could've told me, so I wouldn't think nothin' crazy."

"Come on now, O. You and I both know you was not about to answer no phone for at least thirty minutes, ya fuckin' thot ass nigga. Hold up a sec," Kayla told him. "Yes, please. Custard sounds good."

"Where did you go?" Omar asked, hearing a voice announce a total price.

"Culver's. I found one on… Green Bay Road and… 52nd Street."

"Aight. Bring me somethin'…"

"*Aahh!*"

Omar stopped mid-sentence when he heard Kayla scream. His dogs started barking viciously. Omar's heart started racing.

"Bitch! Get out the car! Now!" he heard a guy shout a second later, then he heard gun shots.

Brrrrrrrr!

***

The masked shooter fired up into the air. The shots immediately caused panic inside, outside, and even in the two major streets that crossed each other with businesses surrounding the intersection. Smoke and Haze both barked viciously at the shooters, fearless of the automatic weapons. They were ready to protect Kayla at all costs.

Kayla was stuck. She gripped the steering wheel tightly in her hands. The young girl at the pickup window and her co-workers had taken cover inside the serving area of the Culver's. There had been too many mass shootings to not duck when just one shot rang out.

The shooter stood about ten feet or so away from the passenger door of the Shelby pickup, pointing at her. He demanded once again for her to get out. A second later, the lights of an SUV shone into the pickup through the windshield, blinding her. It skidded to a stop a car length away from the Shelby, boxing her in with the abandoned car behind her. Three more shooters jumped out and pointed automatic pistols with drum clips at her, positioning themselves in front of the pickup.

"Who the fuck are these niggaz, man?" Kayla wondered.

"Bitch ass nigga, we ain't finna tell you no mo'! Get the fuck out the truck!" one of the shooters in front yelled.

Suddenly hit with a red-hot rage, Kayla screamed, "Fuck you!" and mashed the gas pedal to the floor.

The shooter to her right started dumping at the passenger's side as the Shelby shot forward. Kayla grabbed Smoke and pulled him down with her, as bullets blew through the passenger windows. Bullets hit the windshield and the grille, but before the three in front could get out the way, Kayla caught all three of them and crushed them between the pickup and their SUV, killing them instantly. Gritting her teeth as the one remaining shooter kept dumping, Kayla pushed her way out of the box and swerved up out of the drive-thru, but not before the rear window exploded from a barrage of bullets shot through it.

"*Kayla!*"

Hearing Omar's voice boom through the speakers just then startled her. She had completely forgotten that he was still on the line.

"Omar! These niggaz is shootin' at me, yo!" she panicked, reaching the exit and flying out of the parking lot.

"Where are you?" he yelled.

Remembering the way she came to get there, Kayla told Omar that she was back on the big street she'd taken to get there, heading back toward where he was.

Just as she fishtailed out of Culver's, she saw headlights turn behind her. She quickly looked back out of the blown out rear window and saw the SUV was on her ass.

"Maaaan, what the fuck! This nigga is chasin' me now, O! On the Homiez, nigga! Lemme find out ya' lil bitch sent them at me, Omar!"

"Kayla, you buggin'! Claudia wouldn't do that! Homiez, yo! Just keep drivin'! Don't stop! We in her whip, and we headin' in your direction!"

Brrrrr! Brrrrrrrrr!

"Fuck!" Kayla cursed, as slugs flew into the Shelby's cab, a few of them hitting the dashboard. "Where's the joints that Ace got in here?" she yelled out to Omar.

"Center console! False bottom! Slide it back!"

60

Kayla kept one hand on the wheel, eyes on the road, weaving around slower moving vehicles, as did the SUV, refusing to give up. She opened the center and tried to slide the trap back but couldn't. She glanced down to see why it was stuck and saw a little switch in the corner. She flipped it, slid the trap back, and saw the Glock inside. The second she grabbed it, she heard a horn blasting.

"Oh, shiiit!" she screamed, realizing she had drifted into the oncoming traffic lane and was seconds away from a head-on collision with a delivery van.

Kayla slammed on the brakes and yanked the wheel to the right, but it was too late. As she slid sideways, the bed of the pickup smacked into the front-end of the van so hard that it spun the Shelby back around, then the pickup flipped and rolled, tumbling over, and over, and over again, tossing Kayla and the dogs around like rag dolls.

***

"Kayla! Kaaylaa!" Omar heard the sickening crunch of metal that followed her screams.

His heart felt like it was stuck in his throat. When she didn't answer, he immediately thought the worst.

"Come on, Claudia! Come on!" he yelled, nearly in tears.

"I am, Omar!" she shouted back with her foot pushing the pedal to the floor, pushing just over ninety miles an hour.

Speeding through very heavy construction on Green Bay Road that had the street completely fucked up, she could only go so fast. A bump at that speed and it was over for her Lambo truck.

The panic that came from his mouth was foreign to her, and it filled her with envy that he was that distraught over one of his 'workers' as she considered Kayla to be. Claudia couldn't understand it at all. Omar was supposed to be hers. She didn't want him to have any feelings for any other woman, not even friendly ones. She had wanted Omar all to herself for as long as she could remember since meeting him.

Temporarily lost in her thoughts, Claudia zoned out for a minute. She was brought back when she heard Omar say, *"Watch out!"*

To her left, an off-road style SUV speeding alongside of her suddenly swerved and smacked into her. She screamed. The Urus started skidding then spinning out of control. Omar held on for dear life, preparing for the horrible crash that was fast approaching. The Lambo truck hit the curb on the northbound side of Green Bay Road and went airborne, flipping in the air until it landed very violently in the front yard of a small house, inches away from the front door.

***

Jerrod laughed after he saw his baby mama's Urus go flying after he side-swiped her with her own vehicle. Not even slowing down, he kept his foot to the floor and raced to get to where Sneaky was to finish what neither of his clown-ass homies, nor he, could. He half regretted not blowing Claudia's head off, then her little fuck buddy's, but he knew he could always come back for her at least. His plan now was to get the pickup truck that had millions in it and get on so that he could shut Claudia the fuck down and all the other dope boys and dope girls, while he assembled a team of killers to enforce his rule on the streets of Kenosha and every other town surrounding it.

Chapter 6

The pain in her legs was unbearable. Blood was in her eyes, dripping from her head. She was stuck, trapped, couldn't move. She heard the dogs whimpering. Smoke and Haze managed to maneuver their big, bulky bodies around the mangled wreck, coming to her side and refusing to leave her.

Kayla could hear what sounded like traffic still rolling, as if nobody was stopping. Through the smashed windshield, she could see gravel. She surmised that she was in a parking lot or a driveway. Mustering what strength she had left, Kayla pulled her stuck limbs free. She screamed in agony, as the pain made her nearly black out, but she refused to just lay there and die. She knew the shooter had to be close. After all of that crazy shit, there was no way he wasn't coming to finish the job, whatever it might be.

She wondered, if somehow, Tuck had sent goons after her all the way in Wisconsin. The thought of it shook her to the core. Her thoughts were then halted when she heard the sound of gravel crunching under someone's shoes.

Kayla went dead silent, but Smoke and Haze started growling. She muttered a curse and tried to shush them, but it was too late.

"Aye, fam! All I want is the money! Give it up and I'll leave you be!" she heard what sounded like a kid shout.

Money? Kayla thought.

"I don't got no money in here, yo!" she yelled.

63

Suddenly, the shooter dropped to the ground in front of the crunched windshield and pointed his pistol right in her face.

"Lyin' ass bitch!" he snapped and took aim at her.

Smoke and Haze went ballistic. Kayla closed her eyes and got ready to be reunited with her cousin, feeling somewhat relieved about it but torn up inside that she would never get to see Omar again.

Pow! Pow! Pow! Pow! Pow! Pow!

Being in the streets a long time taught one a few things, one being the difference between machine gun fire, assault rifles, semi-automatic handguns, automatics, and revolvers. Kayla's eyes popped back open when what she knew were shots from a revolver sounded off instead of automatic pistol fire like the shooter had.

She saw the young nigga still there, but he wasn't moving. Missing half of his head might be the reason why. Smoke and Haze were still barking, but she couldn't tell at who until she heard a man holler out to her.

"Aye! Famo? You aight in there?"

***

After he snuck up on Sneaky and put all six slugs in his head, Jerrod called out to the person in the truck. First, he heard dogs growling, which made him wish he had more bullets. Then, he heard a female's voice.

"I need help!"

"Hold on! I'm comin'! Just don't let yo' dogs bite me, shorty!"

Jerrod tucked the Bulldog and dropped to the ground. The roof was so crunched in that it was going to be exceedingly difficult to get her out, but she had the money somewhere in the vehicle, and he needed it.

He reached in and took her hands then gently pulled her out. She cried in pain, as she came out through the windshield. She was bleeding heavily. When Jerrod saw the dogs crawl out, he right away jumped back, astounded by the size of them and how evil they looked.

"What the fuck?" he gasped, as they looked at him, staring, dead silent, with their clipped ears perked straight up.

"It's cool, yo. They won't hurt you unless I tell 'em to," the girl said. "Help me up! My leg's fucked up, yo!"

Jerrod heard sirens right then. Muttering a curse, he took her hands, eyes on the dogs still, and helped her up. He looked at her and was instantly moved. Even with blood all over her face and a gash on her head, the girl was bad as hell! He could see that she was thicker than peanut butter.

"Okay. We need to go before twelve get here. Is there anyone else in there?"

"No," she told him.

"Anything you need to get?"

"No."

He furrowed his brows. "Nothing at all?"

"Nigga, I said no!"

"My bad. I just heard dude shoutin' 'bout some money before I lit his dumb ass up. Figured you was tryna get away from him cause he was after yo' bag."

She looked at him with a suspicious glare.

"And how do you figure he was after me for money? That could be my baby daddy tryna take my money."

"True. But that lil nigga is a part of the EBK mob that be runnin' wild out here. If he was chasin' you for some gwop, he likely had info that you was holdin' big cake."

"No, I'm not! Now, can we get the fuck on? Cops are comin'!"

"Yeah. Come on."

He led her and the dogs to where the Jeep idled. The street was bare of traffic. News of the highway mayhem had spread. Nobody was coming near that section.

Helping her up into the passenger's seat then letting her dogs in back, Jerrod jumped behind the wheel and peeled off.

"They call me... Beast. What's yo' name?" he asked her.

"Kayla. Take me somewhere wit' a phone. I gotta call my nigga."

"Yo' nigga? Like as in yo' boyfriend?" he questioned.

"As in my nigga! Please don't be nebby, yo! Homiez, I can't deal wit' that shit right now!"

"My bad, Kayla. Just askin'," Jerrod told her then fell silent, as he got away from the scene, mentally cursing about coming away from it emptyhanded.

***

At a BP gas station, far away from the craziness, up at Green Bay Road and Washington, Kayla tried Omar's phone six times with the store phone. No luck. It was going right to voicemail.

"What the fuck, O? You really just left me to die?" Her eyes watered at the thought of her best friend turning his back on her. After all they had been through, the nigga let a bitch come between them in a life-or-death situation.

"You aight?"

Kayla heard Beast's voice. She blinked her tears away before they fell, then she looked at him.

"Yeah. He's comin' to get me. Lemme get my dogs out ya' truck and you can go."

"Naw, I'll wait wit' you til he gets here."

"Yo, just go ahead, man! Damn! I don't even know you, and you annoyin' the fuck outta me!"

"I'd rather annoy you than leave you out here and get got by them EBK niggas. I wasn't raised to abandon no woman, especially one that's far from home."

"How you know I'm far from home, yo? You don't know me!"

"You say yo like every time you finish a sentence. Don't nobody from the Midwest, West Coast, nor the south say 'yo'. That's East Coast shit."

Kayla let out a frustrated sigh. "Don't worry about me, Beast. You the one that splattered a nigga in a driveway," she told him, purposely leaving out what she did to the other three.

"I'm a gangsta, Kayla. Niggas call me Beast fo' a reason. I'm known in these streets, and I be on them EBK niggas asses. I won't stop 'til all they asses is dead!" he declared in a sudden flare up of anger.

"Why do you hate them so much?"

"They blew at my crib, hit my baby mama, hit my son, all 'cause they was too pussy to come see me!"

Hearing about his baby mama and his son tugged at Kayla's heart. It sounded to her like he had suffered greatly and was hurt. Hunting a clique of young, wild ass teenagers was street justice for him. Kayla understood exactly how he felt.

"I'm sorry about your family. Did they…"

"No. They're both dead. I'm not restin' til all them niggas is dead. Fuck the police, especially Kenosha PD, with they racist asses."

Kayla sighed. His pain was so strong that even she felt it.

"Well, I appreciate the lookout, Beast. I got it from here, yo."

He looked at her. "Where you finna go, shorty? You on foot 'n shit."

"I guess to a hotel for the night, then I'ma catch a bus or plane home."

"Where's home, if you don't mind me askin'?""

Kayla looked at him for a second then told him she was from Pittsburgh, Pennsylvania but was in Keno to visit a friend.

"Yeah, you a long way from home, Kayla. Um… what's the chance that I could drive you to a spot to get some sleep at then take you where you need to go tomorrow?"

"Why, Beast? You don't even know me, and I got two dogs that have showed you that they're ready to rip you apart."

He chuckled, looking at the two blue monsters.

"They definitely look like they been plottin' on me, but I can tell that they're trained well enough to not jump if you don't tell 'em to. They some pit bulls or those XL bullies? They big as hell!"

"No. Cane Corso, *Blue Blood Cane Corso* to be exact."

"Blue blood?" he questioned with a raised eyebrow.

Kayla gave him a little bit of knowledge about the extremely rare breed and how it dated back to the 1800s when it was created in Sicily originally, while the blue bloods full name Alapaha Blue Blood Cane Corso was developed in Rebecca, Georgia. She saw his surprised expression when she told him that the breed had a bite of up to seven hundred psi!

"That sounds like enough to crunch through bone… human bone," he said, looking at Smoke and Haze, while they both were still staring at him.

"That would be correct, player," Kayla replied.

"Soooo… how about that ride?"

"Sure, Beast. Just has to be a hotel that lets dogs in."

"I know one."

"And I'm hungry. So are they. I was orderin' food when them lil dickheads came for me. I can't understand why they thought I was holdin'. Them niggaz came prepared, yo. On my dead Homiez, cuz. It's like they thought I had mils in the truck."

"Did you?" he asked, looking at her.

"No, nigga! I don't fuck around," she capped, not needing the stranger to know more about her than he needed to know.

68

"I work a nine to five back home. Me and my nigga was just up here visitin' a friend."

"Well, they must've thought you was someone else. Come on. I'll take you to get food then to the hotel."

Nodding her head, Kayla looked at Smoke and Haze.

"When ya' daddy decide to pick his phone up, I'm lettin' y'all know now, me and that nigga really gon' kick the fair one. Homiez."

Smoke barked. Haze sneezed, then both stood up and wagged their tails.

Kayla got them back inside the Wrangler then limped up into her seat.

"What happened to yo' leg, shorty?" Beast asked, as he got ready to close the door.

"I think I've reached the limit of questions for the evenin', my man," Kayla told him, feeling like she already let the guy in too much. "I just need some food and some sleep. Can we make that happen?"

"Yeah. My bad, Kayla."

He closed her door and hopped in on his side behind the wheel. Starting the engine, he glanced over at her. She yawned, tired as hell. In the back, he heard grunting. Looking in the rearview mirror, he saw both of the dogs were looking at him, locked on him as if they were heat-seeker missiles and he was a human torch. He looked back at Kayla. Her eyes were closing. Putting it in drive, he pulled off. He went over to the Wal-Mart just on the other side of Green Bay Road, got her and the dogs boxes of grilled chicken from the deli area, bottled waters, then took them to a motel that was nearly at the border of Wisconsin and Illinois on Sheridan Road. He paid for her room for the night, walked her and the dogs to the room, and promised to swing past in the morning.

***

69

Jerrod stayed in the Wrangler for a minute, staring at her door. His plan was coming together as the night grew later. He knew that somehow, Kayla was connected to his baby mama but didn't know how exactly. He most definitely planned to find out, and when he did, he planned on squeezing all of them and anyone else that tried to ride for them.

He saw the light turn off through the window. He put the Wrangler in drive and pulled off. Turning a right onto Sheridan to head north into Wisconsin, Jerrod got his phone out and made a call.

"Yeah?" Kid answered, sounding frantic.

"Aye, Knuck, where the fuck is Sneaky 'n 'em niggas at? I been tryna hit they asses up for the past few hours! I put them on 'biz, and now, they just up 'n ghost me?"

"Naw. Fam, it ain't 'een like that. They dead, all fo' of 'em," Knuck told him, sounding filled with forlorn.

Jerrod feigned surprise.

"Whaaat? How?" he asked, cruising along at the speed limit along the dark deserted two-way road.

"They got popped. Whoever they was chasin' got they asses but only Sneaky got shot, but JWop, Wonnie, and Lil Moe got crushed between a car somehow, man. They was at that Culver's on 52nd."

"Wow. What about who they was chasin'?"

"Who knows? Only *they* got left stankin', G. This shit crazy, bro."

"Don't trip. Keep me in the loop. I'ma see what the streets say, and we'll go from there," Jerrod told him.

"Aight."

Jerrod ended the call, then he burst out laughing.

"On 'erythang! Lil niggas is dumb asses, joe! On me! Man, I finna tear Keno the fuck up and get ghost on these bitch ass niggas. But first, shorty finna be my way in to get at Claudia. Yep. And then, I gots to crack her thick ass. I know that pussy gets wet as fuck! Ooo ooo!"

Jerrod laughed at himself then turned up the music. Staying at the speed limit, he headed to get back to his TLP for the night. He needed to get another whip soon because he knew, at some point, the Hellcat Wrangler would be reported stolen, and he wasn't trying to get caught up in it and end up back in one of Wisconsin's whack-ass prisons where clowns, dope fiends, undercover freaks, snitches, and wannabe gangsters acted like they were all tried and true but were really just miserable bums that had no ambition and no real reason to live.

Chapter 7

"Omar? Hey? O? Baby, can you hear me?"

He heard Claudia's voice, but he couldn't see her. He couldn't see anything. But he felt everything, and everything hurt.

"O? Please talk to me! I'm goin' crazy here!"

"Kayla… Kayla… Kayla!"

His eyes shot wide open then. He shot upright where he unknowingly laid. Claudia was at his side. Instantly, Omar saw he was in a hospital room. The bright light made his aching head pound even harder, like his brain was a twenty-two-inch jack-hammer woofer stuffed into the truck of a Toyota Corolla.

"O! Hey! Relax! You're hurt, baby!" Claudia grabbed his shoulders to steady him. "Look at me! Look at me! Come on!"

"Where's Kayla?" he asked, terrified. "Kay! Kaylaa!"

Nurses rushed into the room when they heard Omar yelling. Claudia was hurt by how he was basically ignoring her, not even attempting to ask if she was okay, despite the bloody bandage on the left side of her forehead.

"Mr. Anderson, sir, please calm down!" one of the nurses urged. "You have a concussion! It's crucial that you relax!"

"Where is Kayla, yo?" Omar asked again, not giving a fuck about his health versus finding Kayla.

"Omar… we got into a crash. We never made it to her," Claudia finally told him.

The color in Omar's face nearly drained. He swore his heart stopped. The worst possible scenario filled his mind.

He was filled with dread, picturing his homie, who he had brought into the game, laid out in a pool of blood, gone.

"Is she...?"

"She's not here in the hospital. I described her to the nurse at the emergency room. Nobody came in with Kayla's description," Claudia informed him. "And!" she continued, knowing what was next. "I called the morgue. In the last twelve hours that you've been out, only four bodies came in. Four young dudes in a gang, no females."

Omar finally looked at Claudia. His eyes met hers. He saw hurt and pain in them. They were wet, glistening, full of real sorrow.

"Twelve hours? Wait... So, Kayla's alive?"

"I would bet on it. Yo' girl has that beast in her, from what I could see. She wouldn't be so easily taken out, baby."

"I need to find her!" Omar urged and tried to get up.

The nurses and Claudia stopped him.

"Yo, what the fuck is wrong wit' y'all? My homie is out in this punk bitch town by herself, probably thinkin' I just left her to die! I swear to God, if y'all don't let me up, on my dead Homiez, y'all gon' feel it!"

The nurses backed off, seeing the blazing fire in his eyes. Claudia, taken aback by his threat, felt tears run down her face.

"Omar?" she spoke, voice breaking.

"Look, Claudia, Kayla is my people. I brought her out here to get away from the drama in our neck of the woods. I refuse to lay here when she could be hurt or snatched up! I need my phone! I bet money she been tryna call me, Claudia!"

Claudia got up from her chair. He watched her go to a table with a vase filled with fake flowers under a big HDTV. He saw his clothes folded on the table. His phone was with them. She grabbed it and brought it to him. Omar went into it and went to the last call.

His people back home had called multiple times. He had their contact info saved, but as he scrolled down, he saw multiple missed calls from a gas station around the time that the crash happened. Immediately, he called the number. A young woman answered after two rings. Omar asked if a woman matching Kayla's description was there or had come in recently. The chick told him no. He then asked where the store was located. Once she told him, he ended the call.

"Take me to the BP on Green Bay and Washington! Now!" he demanded of Claudia.

**

The Uber driver stopped in front of the store. Omar had the door opened before the wheels even came to a stop and hopped out. Claudia, on her phone, made calls to her store's manager to keep it closed for the day then to her distributors to tuck in until she gave them word.

Inside the store, Omar went to the ATM, withdrew as much cash as the machine would allow, then went to ask for the manager. Claudia was right behind him, staying close, ready to do whatever he asked but still jealous that this was all over another woman.

Omar recognized the cashier's voice as the chick on the phone when he asked for the manager, and her response was that she was the manager.

"I'm the one that called earlier! I gotta find my homegirl, Ma!" Omar pulled out five new hunchos and set them on the counter. "I need you to show me the video from ten-thirty to eleven last night!"

"Are you a cop?" the girl asked with a raised eyebrow.

"Bitch, does he look like a fucking cop?" Claudia spazzed, stepping up on Omar's side. "Yo ass got five hundred bucks in front of you to show us a minute worth of security footage! Take it or get beat the fuck up!"

Before the girl could hop to it, Omar's phone started ringing. He saw Chante was calling. Stepping away, he answered hesitantly, thinking that it was more than just him looking for Kayla.

"Y-Yo?"

"Nigga, you must be outta ya' muthafuckin' mind, ghostin' my homegirl like you did, yo! What the fuck is ya problem, O? How you just gon' leave Kay hangin' when she needed you?"

"Chante, I didn't! On the Homiez, I was enroute wit' my partner, Claudia, and some clown ass nigga hit her whip and sent us flippin'! I woke up in the hospital, and now, I'm here where Kayla was tryna call me from to see where she went and how! Homiez, cuz, you know I would never get down on her like that! How the fuck is you accusin' me of that shit?"

"Well, that's what she said, my man. And she's pissed!"

"Hold up... You talked to her?"

"Duh!"

"Where is she? I'll go to her right now!"

"Naw, nigga, chill out. We out here wit' her. We gon' handle the biz. Stay wit' cha lil bitch. We got this."

"Chante! Yo! Hello?"

The call ended. Omar tried to call her back, but the phone just kept ringing. He tried again. The phone went right to voicemail.

"Fuck, yo!"

He tried calling Jerrica. Voicemail. He tried Valerie. Same result. Claudia approached and touched his shoulder. She heard the whole thing and knew Omar was pissed.

"Come on, O. We'll figure it out. Let's get outta here," she suggested.

Reluctantly, he allowed Claudia to pull him out of the store, leaving the manager with a look of shock and confusion etched on her face and five hundred dollars in front of her.

Hopping back into the same Uber, Claudia gave him the address to her babysitter's house, then he pulled off. Omar leaned back in his seat. His head hurt, he was starving, worried, and pissed as shit. Claudia reached over and caressed his cheek.

"Relax, baby. Please?"

"How, Claudia? My best friend thinks I did her wrong! She just got shot two days ago because of me!"

"I understand, but you found out that she's alive, means she's well enough, somewhere, that her emotional state is still intact. So, again, I need you to relax before you fuck yourself up even more."

Omar shook his head. "I can't relax, Claudia."

"Yes, you can! I'll help you," she told him then reached over to undo his jeans.

"Clau…"

"Shhh! If you even think about tryin' to stop me, O," Claudia warned, as she pulled his dick out, "you will regret it."

She repositioned herself on her knees, hunched over him, and opening wide, Claudia took his hardening cock into her mouth, going balls deep with her ass tooted up high.

"Ohh, sssshhhhit," Omar groaned, eyes rolling to the back of his head, feeling her plump lips wrap around him and her hot, wet mouth.

"Hey! You can't do that in my car!" the Uber driver said, glancing in his rearview mirror.

"Shut the fuck up and drive, nigga!" Omar groaned out, as Claudia deep throated his dick. "Mind ya business and you'll get a tip plus good reviews!"

"Well… okay," the driver agreed then put his eyes back on the road, while Omar reached around Claudia, lifted her skirt up, and caressed her magnificent ass through the fabric of her pantyhose, enjoying her phenomenal oral skills.

***

Kayla shook her head. She just couldn't believe it. Her best friend in the world had abandoned her in a state that was foreign to her. He even abandoned his dogs! For what? A thick, white bitch that had dick sucking lips and moved dope for him?

"I'ma beat that nigga's ass when I see him, yo," Jerrica proclaimed.

"Homiez, me too," Valerie swore.

"Me first," Chante added, still pacing back and forth in the small, ratty, trailer park motel room. "O is foul, yo. Real rap."

Sitting on the bed in fresh clothes, a freshly bandaged leg, and feeling no pain from the Percs, Kayla stroked behind Smoke's ears, while Haze laid stretched out by where Jerrica and Valerie sat at the edge.

"What's the deal wit' this new nigga though, Kay? You trust him?" Chante asked, finally stopping and looking at her.

Kayla looked at her homegirl. She was clad in tight jeans, a t-shirt, and Jordans, like Jerrica and Valerie were. She looked at all three of her girls – gangstresses with pretty faces, guns, and they all could scrap like street fighters. Kayla was proud of her crew. She just wished Shay was there too.

"The only nigga I ever trusted was O," Kayla told her with a look on her face that made Chante understand what she was saying.

"So, what's the plan? Cause this nigga said he's a few minutes away, yo,' Jerrica added.

Kayla laid it out for them. Her plan flowed after she thought about what he said would be happening in a few days, but as far as what she had in mind for the day, once she put it out there, her homegirls nodded.

"Period. I'm ready, yo," Chante spoke.

Jerrica got up and went to the duffel bag sitting on the table by the window that had come all the way from the Steel City. She and Chante and Valerie rode out to Wisconsin asap in her Speed edition Bentley Bentayga. When Kayla called her on the motel's phone and told her what happened, she went to sleep and woke up just over seven hours later to her girls knocking on the door, coming to her rescue with clothes, shoes, and a few party favors.

She brought the bag and set it on the bed. Unzipping it, Jerrica revealed the contents. The girls looked inside, and they all began salivating like a greedy clown discovering a treasure chest full of gold and diamonds.

Knock! Knock! Knock!

Jerrica quickly put the bag on the floor. Chante, with a Glock 21, went to the door. Looking out of the peephole, she saw a tall, dark, and very handsome man with a bald fade, waves up top, and a neatly trimmed and lined goatee.

She undid all three locks, gripping the steel with her hand behind her back. Chante opened the door. His eyes went wide in surprise at first when he saw her. Smoke and Haze were growling right behind her until Kayla called them back to her.

"Well, damn. A nigga was only expectin' to see Miss Kayla and the dogs, but this is a nice surprise," he said with a chuckle.

"Yeah, uh huh, all that. Bring ya ass up in here, homie," Chante demanded.

Raising his hands up to signify he came in peace, he stepped inside of the little motel room, feeling like he more so had just entered a den full of hungry lionesses.

***

Jerrod heard the door shut behind him, then the locks reapplied. He saw Kayla on the bed and in new clothes with the Cane Corsos. With her, he saw an amazingly gorgeous chick with skin the color of dark chocolate candies with cherry filling.

The other girl, a light brown-skin chick that had distinctively beautiful looks and dark, wavy hair, sat at the edge of the bed. The girl that opened the door stepped in front of him. She had skin like butter toffee and hair that was dark at the roots but turned a deep reddish toward the ends. She seemed to be the tallest of them all.

"Hands up, my man," the girl demanded.

Jerrod saw her hand come from behind her back. A Glock was in it.

"Okay. Don't shoot, lil mama. I come in peace," he told her, giving her a cheesy smile.

He raised his hands. The girl patted him down and found the FN Five-seveN that he had tucked in the front of his waistline. She took it out and handed it to the dark-skinned chick.

"I will need that, just so you know," Jerrod told her.

"That's if you walk up outta here, player. Go stand over there, yo," the girl demanded.

Doing as told, Jerrod went and stood in front of Kayla. She looked at him through narrowed eyes. The dogs grilled him as well. He had all eyes on him, and for a second, he regretted coming there without a few of his guys as back up. The women in the room did not look like they were for no bullshit, let alone the dogs still looked like they wanted to eat him.

"Sooo… It kind of feels like I'm the enemy right now," he spoke, looking at Kayla.

"Are you?" she asked him.

"No. EBK is."

"And what exactly is 'EBK'?" the dark-chocolate belle asked.

He looked at her. "Every Body Killa. Comes from Chicago, like all the other mobs around the way.

"And you're gon' help us go see them niggaz, huh? What's ya' price, my man?" the girl with the Glock asked.

"My price? Backup, I got plenty money," he capped. "What I need is revenge for my baby mama and my son. Havin' what looks like a group of killers on my side to make that happen is more than a big bag of money to me."

"And then what?" Kayla asked him. "What chu' gon' do after we spank them niggaz?"

"Spank?" Jerrod questioned, having never heard that term before.

"Nigga, play dumb if you want! Answer her question!" Glock girl demanded, cocking her pistol.

"I'ma move in on their blocks. I'ma find me a connect on some good coke, some good dope, and I'ma check into cash. Any more questions?"

Kayla smirked at him. "Naw."

"Good. Now, what all is y'all willin' to do cause even though these lil niggas is young, dumb, and full of cum, they still bout that pistol play. But you saw how I get down. On what though?"

"Whatever it takes, we gon' do. Fuck it. Plus, yo, you came to my aid. I'm grateful for that, Beast," Kayla replied.

Jerrod almost forgot that he told her that was his nickname. He chuckled at himself.

"Ain't shit, shorty. The enemy of my enemy is my friend. Now, let's see these lil' niggas and make 'em run like chicken wit' a wolf chasin' after them."

Chapter 8

"Wooo! Damn! Suck this dick, baby!" groaned Ace, as the freaky Nubian queen sloppily deep throated him in the front seat of his blue Freightliner M2 flatbed tow truck.

He palmed her juicy ass, squeezing on it, smacking it, loving how soft it felt. She was going in on him, deep throating his nine-inch piece with ease, moaning like he was the tastiest treat she had ever had in her mouth.

Rich Gang's *Tap Out* bumped from the system he had wired up inside the cab himself. Ace picked the chick up from her job, downtown at a clothing store. She came out looking like a business class model in a black and yellow, leather, checker-squared, Louis Vuitton dress that fit her like a second skin, and down her glistening legs, on her feet, were yellow, pointed-toe, Louis Vuitton pumps. Her hair was pulled up into a sophisticated bun, and Gucci glasses framed her beautiful angular face, while gold hoop earrings dangled from her ears.

The second she hopped up into his expensive tow truck, which had a finished customer's vehicle on the bed, covered with a tarp, ready to be delivered, she was on it. Before he even got the chance to put it in drive, she had his dick out, was on her knees in the seat, and giving him the best neck ever. It was so good that he had to pull over before he nutted so hard that he crashed.

"Ohh, shit! I'm b-bout to buss! Oooo, ssshhit!"

She sucked harder and faster, using a hand to jerk him at the same time. She tasted his pre-cum, felt his cock swell up in her mouth. His hand squeezed her ass even tighter, then he exploded in her mouth. She kept on sucking until he was empty, and her mouth was full.

"Goddamn!" Ace cursed, as she sat upright in the seat. "You just went bananas on me, Shatonya. That's how you feel?"

Shatonya smiled, then she opened her mouth, so he could see his nut was still in her mouth. Some of it dribbled down her chin and spilled onto her chest.

"I guess so," he chuckled.

She swallowed then.

"Don't be mad at me 'cause I'm a freaky chick, Ace," she spoke with a harmonious tune that made him desire to hear her step into a studio with Ella Mai and Queen Naija. "I told ya ass what I was about when we met at the club."

"True!" he laughed. "I'm definitely not mad though. Never that, Ma. A nigga just… wowed by how open you is wit' me, 'yah mean?"

"Because it's real how I feel about you, baby. Now, let's go deliver this car, so we can go home and enjoy some us time."

Nodding, Ace put it in drive then pulled off from where he was parked on the side of downtown Pittsburgh's Boulevard of Allies with the on-ramp to the Parkway ahead of him.

***

Ace arrived at his customer's meeting place in the Water Front shopping area of Homestead. Pulling up to where he was parked toward the edge of the parking area of Dave & Buster's, Ace came to a stop and got out, excited to show the customer their expensively decked out ride.

Shatonya got out to be at his side, supporting her dude like a real woman should. Ace unchained the vehicle, worked the levers to tilt the bed, then released the chain winch so that the whip rolled off the bed to the ground. The customer, giddy with glee, waited for his vehicle to be uncovered. When it was, he grew googly-eyed at the sight of his glossy, gun metal gray, 1988 Olds G-Body Cutlass, restored from the frame up. Ace tossed the man the keys and opened the door for him. All too readily, he slid up into the new, gray, button-tuck, leather interior with the suede-ceiling, T-top roof, and put the key in the ignition. He started up the ridiculously powerful LS7 Corvette engine and got goosebumps when the car shook.

Ace let the man do a few donuts in the lot. While he did, Ace recorded it with his iPhone to upload to a web page for promotional reasons. Satisfied, the man shook Ace's hand then drove his G-Body home, leaving his rental in the lot to pick up later on.

***

"Ace Customs, can I help you?" he answered when he got a call on his work phone.

"Hi, yeah, I need a tow. Are you available?" a woman asked.

Ace heard Shatonya smack her lips. She wanted to go home with him, not go on another job. Ignoring her, he told the lady that he was and asked where she was. She told him, and he was happy that she wasn't too far away from his shop. Ace gave the woman an E.T.A. then ended the call.

"I can drop you off real quick, bae, and after I…"

"No! Uh uh! Not happenin', Ace!" Shatonya cut him off and put her seat belt on. "I am comin' with you. You're gonna pick the bitch's car up, take her wherever, then we are going home, nigga! Do you understand what I'm sayin'?"

Ace chuckled. "I do, love. Glad to have my ride or die freak ridin' wit' me."

***

"Ohh, damn! Oooweee, yo!"

Arriving in the Edgewood area, Ace saw the late 90's model BMW 750iL sitting on the side of Braddock Avenue, directly under the westbound overpass of the I-376 Parkway. The four-way blinkers were flashing, the hood was up, and standing next to the dark-colored sedan were two white women – one a platinum blonde, the other a ginger red head. Both wore the sluttiest black latex mini-dresses with black fishnets, black thigh-high platform stiletto boots, and sported gothic-style makeup.

Ace's dick twitched in his Dickie work pants. The only thing he loved almost as much as beautiful Black women were white chicks that looked like the rave type that loved getting drunk, high, and dicked down for hours.

"Fuck they think they is?" he heard Shatonya complain, as he made a U-turn and turned on his orange strobe lights.

"Probably was on the way to a party, bae," Ace replied.

He pulled in front of the big body then backed up to it, parking. Telling her to wait inside, Ace got out to go greet his customers.

***

"Ladies? Lookin' real festive tonight," he told them with a lust-filled grin.

"We were enroute to a party, and my car cut off," the blonde informed him. "My name is Lisa, and that's my friend, Kristen. Thanks for coming... uh?"

"Ace. Lemme take a look under the hood."

He grabbed a flashlight and looked around in the big engine bay, inspecting the 5.0 litre V12 engine. He saw nothing out of the ordinary, so he went to try to start it. Ace heard the sounds that came from a bad starter. He informed the ladies of his guess then suggested that he tow them to his shop and allow him to swap the starter. They agreed then accepted an invite to go join his chick in the cab.

Ace got the car onto the flatbed, chained down, then got back up in the cab behind the wheel, immediately receiving a dirty look from Shatonya with the two dominatrix chicks in the rear of his crew cab.

***

At his garage, Ace backed the flatbed to the garage bay door. They all got out of the Freightliner and waited, as Ace got the 750iL off of the truck. Minutes later, he had it inside, parked in a service bay next to where a G-Wagen was up off of the ground on a hydraulic lift.

"Ladies, I have a waiting room if you'd like to get off of your feet. Refreshments are available as well," Ace told them then asked Shatonya to show them the way, while he got to work.

He again ignored her agitated lip smacking and went to his tool/parts room where he had a surplus of parts for a variety of foreign vehicles, old and new. The blonde and the ginger head grabbed their leather handbags from the car and followed the mad Black woman toward the waiting room.

***

Shatonya gritted her teeth, as she pushed through the door that led to the hallway where the waiting area was at the end of.

"Oh! Shit, I forgot my phone in the car," the ginger said just then. "I'll be right back."

She turned back around and scurried off, back toward the garage. Shatonya went to protest, not wanting her dude to be alone with a shmutt.

"She'll be right back, Miss. Don't worry," the blonde spoke up. "I could really use a drink though."

Groaning, Shatonya turned back around and went to continue taking her to the waiting room when, suddenly, she was grabbed from behind. A rag that was wet with a strong chemical was clasped over her nose. She tried to scream for Ace but was muffled. She tried to fight, but the strong chloroform-soaked rag had her losing consciousness.

"Go to sleep, bitch. Sleep," she heard the blonde whisper to her, as her vision began to fade.

Shatonya could feel herself being laid down on the ground. Seconds before everything went completely dark, she heard the blonde chick say, "I'm gonna start looking now. She's down for the count. Keep him busy until I find it…"

***

Ace was headed back to the car with the new starter when he heard high heels tapping on the ground. Thinking it was Shatonya, he turned his head with a smile but saw Kristen coming with a smile of her own.

"Oh… everything aight?" he asked, as she walked up to him.

"Yes. I just wanted to watch you work. Something about places like this… gets me… revved up."

Ace saw pools of liquid desire gazing at him. Her smile was now a seductive smirk. She closed the gap between them then surprised the hell out of him when she reached out and grabbed his crotch.

"Oh, whoa, whoa, whoa!" Ace jumped back from her, warding off her forwardness. "I'm s-sorry, but I… I have a woman. The girl that led y'all to the waiting room is…"

"Busy talking fashion with my girlfriend," she cut in, licking her glossy black lips. "They'll be a while. You know how girl talk is. You and I though can have a little fun on the low."

Ace tried to resist her. He took two more steps back. She kept coming with a look of horny hunger in her eyes that refused to be thwarted until satisfied.

"Kristen! Yo, hold up! You're my customer! It's... it's against policy to fuck customers!" he told her, backed up against a wall now.

"Hmm. Good thing that the plan is for me to stuff that big, black cock of yours down my throat then, huh?" she told him then aggressively undid his pants.

Ace was stuck between a hard place and a bad bitch with a hard dick. She fell to her knees, looking up at him, licking her lips, as she took his boxers down with her. His bone-hard length made her mouth water at the very sight of it. Powerless to her, Ace could do nothing but watch as she wrapped one hand around the base of him then put her lips to the tip, kiss it, then she opened her mouth, stuck her tongue out, and ran it along the side of his hardness.

When she got down to his balls, she raised his dick up out of her way and started licking all over his nuts. Ace groaned when she began jerking his shaft. Mixed with the sensation of her pleasing his sack, he groaned gutturally, head leaned back, eyes closing. He felt her lick back up to the tip of his dick a second later. She opened wide and engulfed all of him with ease. His toes curled up in his Tims as she started sucking.

"Shit! Goddamn!"

Saying fuck it to himself, Ace grabbed the back of her head and started fucking her mouth. He made her gag, but she didn't protest. He wrapped her hair around his hand, pulled her head back, taking his dick out of her mouth. He smacked her face with it. She spit a mixture of saliva and pre-cum out and let it dibble down her chin, then Ace stuffed his cock back into her mouth.

With both hands, he fucked her face like it was a pussy. His balls slapped against her chin over and over again. Minutes later, he felt himself ready to bust his nut. Toes curled, eyes squeezed shut, head back, Ace did everything he could to keep from roaring out loud. He came so hard in her mouth that his knees grew weak. With his eyes still closed, he reveled in the feeling of her sucking him dry. But then…

Click-clack.

Hearing a sound that could not be mistaken for anything else in the world, Ace's eyes popped open, only to discover a big Glock just inches away from his face.

"What the… *Aagghh*! Aye, get the fuck off!" He shouted when Kristen bit down on his dick with her teeth.

"Shhhh!" the blonde told him. "The more you fight, the worse it will be. Nod your head if you understand what I'm saying."

***

Amber saw him nod his head rapidly. She could only imagine the pain he was in with his dick clenched between Cammie's teeth.

"Good job," Amber spoke. "Now, this can be just a simple robbery or a murder. Your choice."

"T-Tell this b-b-bitch to let me go!" Ace stammered.

Cammie bit down even harder.

"Aaaaggghhhh!"

"She doesn't like being called a b-b-bitch," Amber laughed. "Cammie, let him go."

She obeyed without debate. Standing up, Cammie hawked a wad of spit and cum in Ace's face, then she punched him in his nuts so hard that he screamed and farted at the same time.

Ace was in agonizing pain, and Amber couldn't help but laugh at how pathetic the so-called dope-man-of-Homewood's right hand looked, curled up in a fetal position. Cammie got on her job and found an electrical cord on the tool table. She quickly tied Ace's wrists and ankles, while he was incapacitated.

Amber then had Cammie go get Ace's chick, while she stood over him, watching him writhe in pain and looking up at her with fire in his eyes.

"You can be angry all you want, Ace. You all know that this is all part of the game you play. So, let's play," she told him with a vicious, shit-eating grin.

Cammie returned, dragging the tied-up Shatonya behind her by her tied ankles, wrists bound, mouth gagged. Amber saw Ace's eyes go wide with fear when he saw his chick being dragged in, barely conscious.

"Who the fuck are y'all, yo?" Ace asked, stupefied that a couple of white shmutts got the drop on him and his chick so easily.

"We're friends… of your enemy," Cammie answered. "We'll make it simple, Ace. We know you hold and move coke and heroin for Omar. We know you have a major stash here. Give it up and the money or your whore will experience a death that is very uncommon to anyone from the hood. Hell, anywhere for that matter."

"I do not move drugs, yo. Y'all buggin'," Ace replied, not at all convinced that the women weren't cops.

Amber sighed. "I knew it. I fucking knew it. Cammie, show him that we are not playing."

Ace, with a rapidly beating heart, watched as the ginger head went over to where his big air compressor tank was. She grabbed an air hose, connected one end, and cut the other off with a pair of wire cutters. Finding a roll of Gorilla tape, she brought the hose and tape over to where Shatonya laid.

"Yo, yo, yo! What is you doin'?" he panicked.

Cammie stuffed the hose in Shatonya's mouth, then ignoring his pleas for her to be left out of it, she began wrapping the strong tape around Shatonya's mouth and head, so no matter what… the hose would not come out.

"*Aye*! No! Chill out, yo! Come on!" Ace pleaded.

"You know you fucked up, right?" Amber said to him, chuckling.

Cammie went to the compressor, and she turned it on.

"*Noo*! Stooop! Stooop! Pleeaase!"

Shatonya began regaining consciousness at that moment. She heard Ace's shouting, then realizing that something rubbery was in her mouth, stuck, and that her wrist and ankles were bound tightly, she started panicking.

"*Shatonya!*" Ace cried in sheer terror.

Cammie pushed the handle to the compressor down just as 135 psi of compressed air had been crammed into the big tank. Ace saw the hose flipping and flapping. Air was flowing from the tank into Shatonya's mouth. She shrieked as it began blowing her head up like a helium tank did a balloon.

"*Okay*! It's all in the tool room! All of it!" Ace yelled, literally seeing Shatonya's head expanding.

Cammie did not push the lever back up. Amber just stood there. Shatonya cried in agony.

"*Stoooooop*! I told you what you wanted to know! Please!"

"It's too late, tough guy," Amber told him. "Plus, I am dying to see what happens next!"

Ace looked over at his chick, defeated. Three seconds later, as she thrashed and kicked around...

Pop!

Her head exploded from the pressure. Bloody chunks of brain and pieces of skull flew all over the floor. The strong whoosh of air now flowed freely through the bottom of her jaw.

"Whoa! Holy shit! That actually worked?" Amber exclaimed, wide-eyed with astoundment.

Cammie shut the compressor off and looked at her roadie with an evil smirk.

"You doubted me?"

"A little. Guess you showed me," Amber chuckled.

Ace was stuck. He couldn't take his eyes off Shatonya's headless body. He could barely even breathe.

"Go check the tool room, Cammie. It's time for us to finish up," Amber directed.

Watching the ginger dip off, Ace felt his whole world crashing down. He had a few million dollars' worth of cocaine and heroin in the tool room, not counting the cash that was rubber banded, wrapped in plastic, ready to go to the connect for the re-up. Omar was going to be pissed!

"You ain't gon' get away wit' this, bitch," he told the blonde, grilling her with a fiery glare. "On Crip, you gon' die!"

She turned and looked at him. "Did you not just see how your bitch just died? You have the nerve to talk shit? You are a dumbass."

Amber shook her head, tisking at his stupidity. Cammie came back through the tool room door and gave her a thumbs up. She walked toward Ace and grabbed his ankles. He tried to kick loose from her grasp, threatening her in every way humanly possible. She ignored him and dragged him under the raised lift that had the Mercedes truck on it.

"Time to join your bitch, Ace," Amber said to him, stepping away, while Cammie went to the control levers.

"Fuck you! Bitch! I swear to God, on my dead homiez, y'all gon'…"

Cammie hit the lever to the lift. More than two tons of G-Wagen dropped down and smashed Ace like a pancake. His feet stuck out from under the lift, both twitching for a few seconds then going still.

"Alrighty then. Let's get the shit and burn this place down," Amber told her partner.

"Why can't we just get the shit and go?"

"You sucked his cock and spit in his face, genius! Your DNA is all over him! Stop sucking every guy's dick before we kill him, and we might not have to! Slut!"

"You suck as much dick as I do, so shove it, whore!"

Amber glared at Cammie. Cammie scowled at Amber. Then, a second later, they both burst out laughing.

"Oh, my God! Now that was funny! Let's finish this job and get the rest of our money. Then, we find Omar and put him down."

Cammie shook her head at that.

"Since Omar is such a high target for that cocksucker, then we're gonna need more money. $25,000 doesn't seem like enough. A quarter million is more like it."

"Ooooo, my dear love, I do love the way you think!" Amber replied, then the two 'cleaned up' after themselves and got up out of there, ready for the last half of their job.

Chapter 9

The two-story apartment building near the dead-end of 20th Street by 57th Street jumped as the lit-up house party inside of it cracked. It was filled with ballers and young, lusty chicks trying to catch one however they could. The EBK mob was getting money around Kenosha, and everyone knew it. Get in their way, step on their toes, they came for you, deep as hell with switches and drums, leaving no witnesses.

EST Gee blared from the big house speakers wired up in the big living room. It was filled with potent smoke from exotic weed, bottles of pricey liquor, and all sorts of pills being popped or crushed and snorted.

Natalie squealed as she felt the ecstasy pill being put up her asshole by the EBK goons' big homie. The tiny skirt she chose for the baller party was up around her waist. Her amazingly plump ass, emphasized in the fishnet pantyhose she had on, now with a hole ripped at the back, had Knuck dying to hit it from the back.

With the cute little Mexican chick was a thick-ass redbone that was garbed in a tight-ass dress that was made completely of see-through lace material. Under it, she wore a bra and a thong, and on her feet were slutty red pumps with pointed toes and six-inch heels. Knuck had immediately locked onto Natalie's friend because she strongly resembled the rap chick, Ice Spice. She even had the crazy curly afro the celeb so famously rocked, along with the voluptuously curvy body that had niggas' eyes go wide when they saw all that ass she had.

"Shit, nigga!" Natalie cursed, fanning herself, as the pill Knuck put in her ass immediately started taking effect. "That shit got me feelin' wild as hell! I'm ready to fuck!"

"Straight up!" Jessica chimed in, sitting on the edge of Knuck's big bed, legs crossed, pussy wet as hell, and her clit throbbing, yearning for some stimulation.

The brown-sugar toned Knuck, 5'9" tall, built like an athlete, tatted up, had his shirt off, revealing his chiseled and tatted physique, while his fitted Balmain jeans sagged lower than normal. His long dreadlocks hung loosely, as did the two long diamond-encrusted Cuban link chains hanging from his neck. One had EBK as a charm and the other, a Jesus piece. The Rolex on his wrist was fitted with flawless diamonds as well, flicking so hard like they were made of light.

He wasn't even twenty-one yet but had bank rolls, cars, a house, trap spots all around Kenosha, and loyal goons that asked how high when he told them to jump. Knuck was that nigga out in the streets, and it wasn't shit for him to bump two or three freaks that didn't mind sharing.

"Sheit, let's get it poppin' then," Knuck told them, ready to pound both their asses out.

He undid his pants and dropped them with his boxer briefs. Natalie and Jessica all but ran to him, as he pulled his bone-hard, nine-inch tool out. Without even being told to, they dropped before him and got to it.

Natalie grabbed his cock and started licking all over it. Jessica put her face under him, kissing and licking his hairy balls. Knuck groaned deeply, as he felt the two working in sync to please him. He watched with sheer glee, as Natalie opened her mouth wide and took him into her mouth right as Jessica took his balls into hers and sucked on them. Knuck's eyes rolled to the back of his head. His toes curled in his Timberlands. He cursed, as the pleasure, enhanced by the liquor, weed, and molly he had partaken in, nearly crippled him from how good it felt.

Natalie spit his cock out a second later. Jessica released his nuts, then the two rose up on their high-heeled feet. Natalie got up on the bed, as Moneybagg Yo came on. She got on all fours and looked back at him, pursing her shiny red lips. Jessica got up in the bed next to her. She grabbed her homegirl's ass cheeks and spread them, opening her wide for Knuck to go in.

Knuck's dick throbbed even harder when he saw Jessica lean down and lick Natalie's asshole. He bit his bottom lip, grabbed his dick, and stepped forward. She spit on Natalie's asshole next. As Knuck scooted up behind the Mexican, Jessica took his hardness in her hand and rubbed the tip in her saliva, lubing Natalie up for him. Then, she put his tip to it, and Knuck gently eased inside.

"¡Aayy!" she cried out when he began stroking her.

Knuck cursed. He grabbed her hips, as he pushed all the way in then out. As he stroked, he heard what sounded like loud popping sounds, but he was feeling way too good to care about anything else then.

Jessica positioned herself on her back in front of Natalie. She opened her legs wide. Knuck kept fucking Natalie's ass but watched as she started sucking Jessica's pussy, slurping loudly, making Jessica moan out and grab her breasts, rubbing them. Knuck felt his nut rising minutes after they started. His back muscles got tight as did his nuts. He groaned out loudly, threw his head back, closing his eyes as it rose even higher. A second after, as he pulled out of Natalie, he exploded. Grabbing his cock with his left hand, he jerked it and skeeted all over her ass cheeks. At the same time, Jessica climaxed, squirting Natalie in her face.

"Bring yo thick ass here, shorty," Knuck said to Jessica, dying to fuck the shit out of her too.

All too eager for the dick, the curly French fry head belle got up and got on all fours, tooting her ass up high for him while putting her face down low. Natalie smacked Jessica's ass while looking at him, giving him a sexy fuck face before she opened her up and spit down into her crack. She rubbed her saliva all over Jessica's asshole for him when…

Bam! Bam! Bam! Bam!

Someone started pounding on the door, interrupting Knuck's real live fantasy.

"Get the fuck on!" he yelled as Natalie put her finger in Jessica's asshole. "We busy in here!"

"Kenosha Police Department! Knuck, we know that's you in there!"

Knuck immediately fell backwards off the bed and scrambled to get his pants up. The girls did the same, scared as fuck, knowing Kenosha had trigger-happy cops and that Knuck was a high-priority target that would not go down without a fire fight.

"Knuck!"

Bam! Bam! Bam!

"Open up or we're comin' in!"

"Knuck! What do we do?" Natalie asked frantically.

"Sheeit, I know what I'm finna do!" he shot back just as they all heard loud gunshots from outside the bedroom.

Boom!

The door exploded into pieces, as he got to it. Knuck raced over to his window where a fire escape was. The girls, who were scared shitless, both screamed and dove to the floor. He couldn't help but look over at the doorway, but as he did, he saw that it wasn't cops coming through. His eyes went wide as dinner plates when he saw Jerrod step in, wearing all black, gripping a FN Five-seveN in his hand.

"Nigga, what the fuck?" Knuck demanded, dumbfounded by Jerrod's presence.

"You in my way, Knuck. A nigga's hungry. I finna eat yo' food, bitch ass nigga," Jerrod replied with a diabolical smirk, then he raised the semi-auto up at him. "Y'all say EBK, but I really am gon' kill everybody!"

Knuck cursed and flew the coop, jumping out of his window onto the fire escape. He heard Natalie and Jessica scream just then. Four gunshots came. Their screaming stopped. Running down the old, iron steps, Knuck realized he forgot the keys to his whip and his phone, and he didn't even have a gun.

"Where you goin', Knuck?!" he heard Jerrod shout out of the window.

Boc! Boc! Boc! Boc!

Four more shots came. Bullets pinged off the fire escape, coming so close to Knuck that pieces of shrapnel hit him.

He jumped the last eight steps and took a tumble before his feet hit the ground. From the main entrance at the side of the door to the apartment, people that had been in his party ran out, screaming and yelling in fear. Gunshots inside continued. He could hear his homies being bucked inside.

"Fuckin' snake ass nigga!" Knuck growled, quick stepping toward a few of his guys that made it out and were hurrying toward a newer GMC Yukon Denali.

Knuck called out to them and got their attention. They yelled for him to hurry up. Sirens wailed out from very close by. It would be only a matter of minutes before the cops showed up. He got to within eight feet of the Yukon when machine gunfire erupted. Bullets slammed into the SUV, lighting it up and killing his guys before they even had a chance to shoot back.

Knuck saw masked shooters standing next to an older S-Class Benz parked toward 57th. The crowd that made it out scrambled in the other direction from the shootings, terrified. Then, one of them opened the back door to the Benz. Knuck's eyes went wide with fear when he saw two huge dogs that looked like demons jump out and run right to him.

"Shit!"

He took off running toward the house at the dead-end, so scared that he pissed his pants on the way. He could hear the dogs coming really fast.

"Come on, come on, come oooon!" he pleaded to his legs, as he ran toward the chain-link fence that was at the rear of the house.

Knuck made it with not even a second to spare. He catapulted himself over it right as the dogs reached it. They both tried to jump over and get his ass, but it was too high for them. He looked into the eyes of the murderous canines, as he sat on his ass in the dirt. They growled viciously, eyeing him like they were thinking of another way. Not even close to trying to give them an opportunity, Knuck got himself up and limped through the dark backyard filled with trees and bushes to get to the other side where 56th Street would be his escape.

***

Jerrod hurried to find any and everything of value that he could in Knuck's room. Cops were coming. The EBK building was already a target for Kenosha PD. He found diamond jewelry, some stacks of cash, two bricks of heroin, and three Glocks all under Knuck's mattress. Grabbing one of the dead girl's handbags, he dumped it all out, stuffed his come up in it, then right before he ran out, he heard dogs barking and growling.

Unable to resist, Jerrod ran to the window and saw Kayla's vicious blue blood killers chasing Knuck. Jerrod's eyes grew eager with excitement, as he rooted for the dogs to get him. He needed Knuck dead anyway so that he could not ever speak his name to any other EBKs that hadn't been there or anyone else. He cursed when he saw Knuck launch himself over the fence just in the nick of time before he got ripped apart.

"Dammit!" Jerrod yelled angrily.

He saw Knuck get up and run into the dark backyard of the house that everyone used as their escape when shit got hectic, and they had to get up out of there.

As sirens got closer, Jerrod looked and saw Kayla and her girls hopping back into the early 2000's model S55 AMG that the dark chocolate girlrilla peeled for the mission. Kayla whistled for the dogs. They ran back to her and jumped in the back. Kayla hopped in the Benz and peeled off, busting a big U-turn and speeding off to 57th.

Jerrod high-tailed it out of the bedroom, running through the sea of dead EBK members and chicken heads that were covered in blood and guts like a bomb had gone off in the living room. He was impressed with Kayla and her clique's murder game. He only wished he could make them his, but Jerrod knew that all that he did in the dark would come to the light; he in no way wanted to be anywhere near her when Kayla found out that *he* was EBK.

Chapter 10

Knuck limped as fast as he could up 56th. Cop cars were everywhere now, flying past him, heading toward the EBK spot. He kept as low as he could, trying to keep any of them from seeing him.

"*Freeze! Police!*" he heard behind him just then.

Knuck cursed, stopping dead in his tracks. Immediately, he thought about when the overzealous Kenosha cops attempted to murder a young, Black man, which set off a chain reaction of World War III type turmoil to Kenosha, all because the cops shot the man in the back.

"Hands up! *Now!*" the cop shouted.

"Aight! Don't shoot! I'm unarmed!"

Knuck raised his hands up and had begun to get down on his knees when demanded to do so when just then, he heard an engine revving high. He looked toward the street and saw the same black Benz the shooters were in coming right for him.

"Oh, shit!" He panicked as it swerved to the right and hopped the curb.

***

Valerie slammed on the brakes and slid to a stop before the AMG's bumper made contact with Knuck's face. Without any hesitation, Kayla jumped out with two Glocks, followed by Jerrica and Chante and the dogs.

"Hey! Hey! Drop your weapons! Drop 'em!" yelled the cop that had been about to slap cuffs on Knuck, pointing his weapon at him.

Smoke and Haze charged him. He let off a shot but missed. Smoke jumped and took him down with ease. He chomped down on the cop's face, while Haze chomped down on his arm. Kayla ran right up on Knuck and swung one of her Glocks on him, cracking him right in his temple, knocking him clean out, then wasted no time in grabbing him by his ankles.

Chante and Jerrica kept their eyes open, guns up, watching Kayla's back, as she dragged Knuck to the back of the Benz. A loud snapping sound ricocheted in the air. The cop's bloodcurdling scream of pain stopped. Smoke and Haze ran to Kayla's side with blood smeared all over their snouts. Kayla muscled Knuck into the trunk, and as fast as she could, she bound his wrists with zip ties she had then tied his ankles with bungee cord.

"Come on!" Valerie yelled, listening to the police scanner she had also brought from Pittsburgh.

She heard Kenosha's central dispatch calling cars over to where they were after an officer's call for assistance went un-replied to.

Kayla, the dogs, and the girls jumped back in the car. Valerie mashed the gas and ran the dead cop over, as she flew off of the sidewalk and back onto the street. No sooner than her wheels touched the asphalt did two Kenosha police cars appear behind her, lights on, flashing sirens blaring.

"Central from Unit 10-11! In pursuit of a black Mercedes going south on 56th!"

Another shouted, "Officer down! I repeat! Officer down! I need an ambulance now!"

They all heard the yelling on the police scanner. They were burned. Besides their exact identities, the cops were on to them. Valerie only had the navigation system as her directions. Not a single one of them had a clue of where they were. Kayla, in the back with the dogs, and Jerrica were heated that Beast had vanished. He had gone inside with the plan to flush Knuck out but immediately started shooting at EBK members. She and her girls had to help him when he quickly got outnumbered. What threw her for a loop was how, before Beast popped the first dude, it seemed like the guy knew Beast and was damn near looking like he was going to dap him up. Then, Beast domed him, then another, and another. The music was so loud, Kayla figured that it was the only reason why Knuck had not bounced right away. Now, they had the EBK goon in the trunk. She wanted answers on why his shorties had come for her, and she was hell bent on finding out.

As Valerie put her driving skills to work, keeping the AMG's gas pedal to the floor, while she swerved around cars, SUVs, trucks, and buses that were unaware of the chaos going on in the vicinity, Kayla pulled her burner phone out and tried to call Beast again. This time, he picked up.

"Yo! Where the fuck are you?" she snapped.

"Maaaan, I'm in the cut, joe! You see how many cops is around? I'm not tryna end up like ol' boy that got popped by the cops in his back cause his baby mama trusted twelve to handle him!"

Valerie swerved hard to the left, tossing everyone and the dogs to the right, as she came close to rear ending another car.

"Fuck was that sound?" she heard Beast ask.

"The fuckin' cops are on our ass, nigga! All you had to do was flush the nigga out! First thing you do is spank a muhfucka!"

He burst out laughing.

"Maaan, I am sorry, but that word be throwin' me all the way off, shorty. Look, I'll meet you at the spot I programmed into yo' navigation."

"Hurry up! I gotta get this nigga out the trunk and in another whip, so we can ditch this one!"

"Hold up… You have him? In the trunk?"

"Muthafuckin' right I do! Fuck, you think I'm not gon' get his ass? There's a reason they call me a girlrilla, my man! You better learn about me! Now, hurry the fuck up and get there!"

Kayla ended the call and angrily cursed. Smoke and Haze, both sitting on the floorboard by her, looked at her with sad eyes.

"Yo, Kay. Homiez, cuz, somethin' is up wit' ya mans," Jerrica spoke up. "Somethin' feels real off about him."

"For real, yo!" chimed in Chante from up front.

"Why not let us just murk his ass and put all worries and suspicions to bed?"

"Because I said so! Now, drop it!" Kayla demanded.

They went silent. The only things that could be heard were the V8 engine under the hood and multiple sirens.

Kayla was suddenly hit with a fit of red-hot rage. Omar leaving her high and dry to die, Beast putting her and her girls in harm's way. Kayla lost her cool at that moment.

"Open the sunroof!" she shouted.

Chante hit the button and made the glass slide back. Kayla grabbed her automatic Uzi and got up. She pulled her hoodie over her head and raised the black bandana she had tied around her neck up to her nose. She stood up through the sunroof, and with her machine gun, she started dumping at the cop cars that were pursuing them.

Relentlessly, she fired at the first car, hitting the cop behind the wheel. He lost control and hit a parked car. She blew at the second car and hit her target. She saw blood splatter on the windshield before it lost control, ran into the oncoming lane, and ran into the front of a store. She lit up the third and fourth and stopped them from continuing to chase them by sending them to the afterlife with their squad members.

Sinking back into the car, Kayla sat back in her spot, dumped the nearly spent clip out, and slapped in a fresh fifty.

Valerie wiped sweat from her forehead, relieved beyond belief to have such a fearless big homie as her friend. Kayla was the bravest and beastiest chick she had ever known, and Valerie was proud to be a part of her girlrilla gang.

"Val! *Look out!*" Chante screamed.

She saw four cop cars skid to a stop in the middle of 56th and 16th Street, blocking her path. She hit the brakes and started skidding. Her eyes then went wide, as she saw the cops hop out with AR-15s. They pointed right at the Benz's windshield. Valerie came to an abrupt stop about forty feet back from the intersection. Frozen, she had absolutely no clue what to do.

"*Fuck!*" Chante cursed.

One of the cops got on a bullhorn and yelled for them to get out of the car with their hands up.

"Should we shoot our way out?" Chante asked Kayla, holding her own Uzi, prepared to go out with a bang if it came to it.

Jerrica had hers and was ready too, as was Valerie.

"No. Them punk ass pigs'll light us up if they even think we gon' hop out and dump," Kayla told them, remembering how Beast had showed her a news clip of when the cops shot a man in his back, which sparked a violent unrest in downtown Kenosha where a bunch of businesses were burned down, including a probation office, during riots.

"Yo, I'm not just gon' go willingly," Valerie chimed in, as the cop shouted his demand again. "All we gotta do is…"

Smash!

From behind, the Benz was rammed by what felt like a damn semi. The girls screamed from the devastatingly hard impact. The Benz went spinning out of control, hitting the curb hard enough that the driver's side wheels broke off.

"Shit!" Kayla groaned, as the dust settled.

Having no clue what had actually just happened, she hurried to look around. Through the shattered rear window, she saw a big pickup careening toward the cop cars. A few of the cops opened fire on it then dove out of its way before it rammed its way through their roadblock. Two cops ran toward her and her girls, guns pointed at the Benz. Smoke whimpered next to her. She noticed he had a cut on the right side of his face. Haze was trapped under Jerrica, who Kayla realized was unconscious.

"No! *Jerr*! Hey!" She reached for her homegirl, shaking her.

Valerie, groaning in pain from her face hitting the steering wheel so hard that she felt like it was broke, turned around and saw Jerrica was unresponsive. Chante, bleeding heavily from cuts on her face from glass hitting her, screamed in fear, thinking Jerrica was dead. Jerrica let out a weak groan as Kayla shook her. She was alive but hurt very badly.

"Everyone in the car! Do not move or we will shoot!" they all heard shouted at them then.

Kayla cursed angrily. They were caught with murder weapons and a tied-up mob nigga in the trunk.

Kayla could hear the cops' footsteps, as they came closer. He continuously swore that if anyone moved, he would shoot to kill. The dogs both growled and barked. A threat to neutralize them if they even so much as looked like they would attack was then issued. Unable to believe they were caught, Kayla's eyes welled up with tears. She felt horrible. Her girls were going down, all because they were riding for her. She was their downfall. It hurt her heart to know that it was all over. The worst part was not ever being able to see Omar again, except through plexiglass or video and visits in a crowed, stinky visiting room in some prison.

"I'm sorry, y'all! I'm so sorry!" she wept.

Flashlights shone into the car from the cops. They issued a demand for them to get their hands up. Nearly ready to surrender, Kayla, Valerie, Chante, and Jerrica obeyed. Smoke and Haze continued growling and barking defensively.

"Once again, do not move an inch until backup arrives, or we will be forced to shoot! Do you understand?"

Skuurrrrr!

Screeching tires filled their ears after the cop's words. Kayla and her girlrillas heard the cops shouting, *"Gun! Gun!"*

Brrrrrrrrrrrr! Brrrrrrrr! Brrrrrrrrr!

The unmistakable thunder of assault rifle fire had the girls all tripping hard. Kayla managed to turn her head to look out of the shattered rear window. A masked man was dumping on the cops with a chopper. They had nowhere to take cover, as their cars were destroyed by the speeding pickup truck.

All four of them dropped when hailstorms of bullets ripped right through them as if they weren't even wearing bulletproof vest. The shooter ceased fire when the last cop's body dropped to the ground. Then, she saw him look towards the Benz.

"Kayla!" he yelled out.

She gasped in the truest shock ever when she recognized the sound of Omar's voice.

***

Omar rushed to the crunched-up Benz. He was overwhelmed with fear that she and the girls were hurt. He heard his dogs barking, which told him that they were alive. Running toward the car with his AK, Omar prayed to God that the girlrillas were alive too.

"Kayla! Oh, fuck!" He got to the car and saw through the blown-out windows that she and Jerrica, Chante, and Valerie were all alive and moving.

"O!" Kayla called out to him.

Smoke and Hase went wild with excitement.

"Hold on! I'ma get y'all out!"

Omar moved fast. He didn't hear sirens yet, but that didn't mean more cops weren't on the way.

All by himself, he managed to get Kayla out, then Jerrica, Chante, and Valerie. Smoke and Haze freed themselves and got right at Omar's side. He got Kayla to the older Toyota Sequoia that he had come to the rescue in, while Valerie and Chante carried Jerrica. With the dogs in the back and the girlrillas safe, Omar ran back to the Benz with his chopper and blew as many rounds as it took to hit the fuel tank.

The Benz exploded in a ball of fire. Omar ran back to the SUV and jumped up behind the wheel. Seeing that the fire was already consuming the interior, he knew that not a single technician would be able to pick up any DNA from any of the girls.

Slamming it into drive, Omar punched the gas pedal and rocketed off, leaving dead cops, a burning car, and no evidence of those he loved most in the world being involved.

Chapter 11

"Dammit! I thought for sure they was gon' get they shmuttie-asses killed," Tuck grumbled after ending the call with Amber. "Now, I gotta pay another twenty-five grand! I can't keep takin' losses out here!"

"Why is you always complainin' about somethin'?" asked Nala, while she rolled up a blunt of Death Star.

Sitting in the front seat of her Range Rover while Tuck brooded in the passenger's seat next to her, Nala could care less of Tuck's troubles in the streets. In her opinion, he brought it upon himself by trying to fix what wasn't broken. Greed killed everyday, and in the process, a lot of innocent people met their demise as well.

Tuck looked over at her. She was licking the tab of the blunt to close it up. He imagined that she was licking him and felt his dick twitch in his pants.

"Come here," he told her.

"No."

"Fuck you mean 'no'? Bitch, come here!"

Nala shrieked and giggled, as he reached over and grabbed her. Putting up a fake fight, Nala acted like she was resisting him, but she wanted him to get rough with her. She got dripping wet from that shit.

Tuck pulled her over onto his lap. Nala swiveled around and straddled him. She looked down into his eyes, as he looked up into hers.

"You love me?" he asked her.

She snorted a laugh. "No, nigga! I don't fall in love, homie! I get money!"

Tuck laughed. "Okay then. Well, soon, that bitch ass nigga, O, gon' be out of the way, and all of the hood will be mine."

Now Nala was the one laughing.

"Fuck is so funny?" Tuck wondered.

Nala grabbed a lighter and flamed her loud up. Puffing on it until it was good and lit, she inhaled deeply. The potent smoke tickled her lungs and instantly had its effect on her. She pulled Tuck's head forward, pressed her lips to his, and gave him a shot-gun kiss.

Tuck inhaled the smoke that she blew into his mouth. His hands traveled around to her plump rear and cupped it. Nala's tongue parted his lips then met his own. Tuck started trying to lift her skirt up, but abruptly, she stopped him and pulled back from the kiss.

"Really? You gon' get a nigga high'd up and make my joint hard, then you gon' pull back?"

Nala chuckled. "You mad?"

"No. I don't get mad, bitch. I'm a player."

"*Ha!* You's a funny nigga, yo."

"Fuck is you steadily laughin' for, Nala? What? You wanna be given an example again of how I get down?"

"Yeah, yup. Do that, Tuck, cause real rap, this move right here that we waitin' on, you think it's gon' be easy. I heard about this nigga though. He likes foolin' people wit' little traps 'n shit."

She took a puff of her blunt, inhaling deeply, then exhaled a thick cloud of smoke.

"Pass that shit, girl! Goddamn!" Tuck growled at her.

"Nuh uh. Roll ya own nol', homie. You ain't put in on this, so ya lips ain't touchin' it. I got somethin' else for ya lips though, boo."

Nala burst out laughing at his face.

"Bitch, I'll slap the fuck outta you, yo."

"Nigga, please," she replied, waved him off, and took another deep puff.

"Bitch," he muttered under his breath then leaned back in his seat, looking at the target's house where Whiz was already inside with the man's wife, waiting patiently for him to get home from work.

***

Omar turned into the stone-paved driveway of an exclusive luxury modern farmhouse down in the Gurnee area of Illinois. It was tucked back from Delaney, the main road, and surrounded by trees and bushes that privatized the three-and-a-half-acre property. It was 7,280-square-feet of A-list celebrity worthy stylings that could rival most mansions that were double or triple the size.

He glared over at Kayla and saw her eyes roaming, likely wondering whose home they were at or thinking they were at Claudia's place.

"Why exactly are we not on a plane to Mexico? Or Japan?" he heard her ask, as he came to a stop at the rounded driveway that sat in front of the house.

"First rule of dippin' from cops. Make sure you *know* that they know who you are."

He put the Sequoia in park then looked at her. "But if they don't and you cleaned up real good after yaself, then hoppin' a plane isn't necessary. Doin' so while bloody as hell would likely make TSA agents follow you. So, we gon' post up here until I get word that we in the clear. This house is off the grid. Trust me."

"Lemme guess… It's…"

"No." He cut her off quick. "It's not Claudia's. It's mine. On trips where I'll be on business for a few days, fuck a hotel. I wanna stay in my own crib."

They both heard shifting around in the backseat. Turning, they saw Chante, Jerrica, and Valerie looking at them. Smoke and Haze had their big-ass heads resting on Chante and Jerrica's laps, laid out, relaxing.

"Y'all need to just fuck and get it over wit', yo," Valerie said to them.

"Homiez, cause y'all asses know y'all want to," added Chante.

"Mmmhmmmm," came Jerrica with twisted lips and a raised eyebrow.

"Hey. Y'all know what's funny?" Kayla asked, looking at them.

"What?" Chante asked.

"Shut up!" Kayla yelled then opened her door and got out.

Omar tried so hard to not laugh.

"Let it out, nigga. Then go get that pussy. You know it's yours, so stop fuckin' frontin', Omar," Jerrica told him, giving him a look that epitomized that women knew best.

He chuckled then. "Let's go inside. There's food, drinks, big bedrooms, and plenty of medical supplies inside for occasions just like this.

***

"No, I haven't heard from him yet. I can only imagine what he'll do when he finds out. Sheit, I'm ready to hit the streets and start sweepin'," Kurt said, as he approached his house on Rodi Road out in Pittsburgh's middle-class area of Penn Hills.

"I'm wit' you, bro. Ace and his woman ain't deserve that. Keep me posted," Banks told him.

"Yup. One."

Kurt started slowing down and made a right turn into his modest, one level, ranch-style house. He rolled up the driveway and parked next to the newer Bentley Flying Spur that he had just bought his wife for her 32nd birthday.

He killed the powerfully upgraded engine under the hood of his 2009 ZR1 Corvette, reached over to the passenger's seat, and grabbed the alligator skin Ermenegildo Zegna satchel that he had brought from his private law firm office.

Before he got out, he tried to call Omar once more. He got the voicemail for the tenth time. Kurt was worried. Omar never fielded calls when it came from business associates that were also childhood friends. Kurt wasn't just Omar's legal counsel and his business investment broker, but he was Omar's homie and had been for a long time.

Kurt knew for a fact that Omar not answering calls and replying to texts and e-mails meant something was up. The last thing Kurt knew was Omar was taking a trip to get Claudia together and took Kayla too. But neither of them were answering either. Something was going on out in Wisconsin. Kurt could feel it and didn't like it.

The recent news about Ace and Shatonya had Kurt feeling sick to his stomach. Ace was a certified goon. He didn't understand how someone could catch him slipping. Whoever it was did him and his girl bad. Omar was going to flip.

Kurt opened his door and got out of his Chevy with the satchel. He closed the door and made his way to the elevated walkway lined by tall bushes and inground L.E.D. lights all the way up to the front door of the lavish home. After he entered the security code on the door handle, deactivating the alarm, Kurt unlocked his door and made entry. The second he stepped inside, he saw his wife, tied up to a chair, in the middle of the living room with a scarf tied around her mouth.

"Francesca! What the fuck?" he gasped.

His wife tried to scream, but the gag in her mouth and the scarf prevented it. Kurt went to run to her but froze when a dark figure in the unlit corner of the adjoining dining room emerged, stepping into the dimmed light.

"What up, Kurt? Lovely house you and ya bitch got," the figure said with a voice that told Kurt that it was a kid.

"Lil nigga, do you know whose house you in? Whose wife you dun' touched?" Kurt asked, dropping the satchel, hand going toward his waist.

"To answer ya questions, yes to both, and for the record, you can up that joint on me if you want to, but that's only gonna make things worse for you."

Kurt saw the youngster didn't have a gun in his hand, nor any other type of weapon. He hurried and snatched the Colt 1911 .45 semi-auto from where it was tucked in the front of his Brooks Brothers suit pants, cocked it, and pointed it at the kid.

"I think things are gonna get bad for you before they do for me if you don't get the fuck up outta my crib!" Kurt barked, wrapping his finger around the trigger.

Bocka!

A deafening gunshot close to his ear made both of Kurt's ears ring. He jumped from the sudden blast, heart racing in his chest. Then, his eyes landed on his wife. Her head was slumped, chin on her chest, blood pouring from the bullet hole in the center of her forehead.

"Francesca!"

Crack!

"Agh!"

Kurt went to run to his wife when a hard metal object struck the back of his clean-shaven head with enough force to open up a gaping wound and send him face first to the floor.

Groaning in pain, Kurt managed to roll over onto his back. He could feel blood leaking from his head. He had double vision but was able to see that the kid was not alone.

***

Tuck stepped into the house behind Nala and her bloody Ruger 5-7. He closed and locked the door behind himself. Looking down at the money-laundering lawyer, Tuck grew enraged with anger.

All the money that he had lost to Omar had very likely run through the man's hands and was spread out to different places of business that Omar owned, funding them. The attorney had once been in the streets, getting money with Omar and his Homewood hustlers, until their status was elevated and organization was created. Positions were bestowed upon Omar's crew. Kurt Turner was street smart and book smart as a youngin', so Omar paid for his schooling, which lead to college and eventually business and law school. With a skilled legal representative and consultant on the team that knew how to bang hammers, a mob of dope boys with enough sense to invest dirty money into different avenues to clean it up couldn't lose.

Whiz came forth and picked up Kurt's gun. He pointed it at the man's right foot and…

Bocka!

"Aaaaaaggggghhhhh!" Kurt cried, as half his foot was blown to pieces.

Tuck stood next to Kurt, watching him cry in agony.

Bocka!

A shot from Nala's Ruger blew the toes on his other foot off. Kurt's bloodcurdling scream affected not a single one of them. It was only the beginning if he didn't act right.

"Yo, my man. Stop all that hollerin' 'n shit, or I'll make my youngins give you somethin' way worse to cry about," Tuck told him.

Kurt forced himself into silence.

"Good job. Now, you should know why we're here, but if by chance, somehow, you don't; this is a robbery. I want access to every account that Omar has; I want the locations of every business that he owns, and I want everything of value that you are holding for him. Give it to me, you get to bury ya wife and have a nice family gatherin' afterwards. Hold back and someone will bury y'all next to each other."

Kurt nodded his head. "O-O-kay! I have e-everything down in the basement! The access info's on my laptop, a-a-and I have a s-safe in my closet! But the safe's r-retina scanner eq-q-quiped!"

Tuck nodded his head then had Nala and Whiz help Kurt up. They helped him to his basement. He nodded his head at where a door in the wall by the bathroom was, then he told Whiz the code he needed to enter into the digital pad lock at the side.

Tuck stood by with his own cannon out. Nala let Kurt go. He fell to the floor, bleeding from his destroyed feet. They watched Whiz enter the code. A 'click' sound came a second later, then Whiz pushed the door and stepped in. The door slammed shut behind him suddenly. Tuck's eyebrows furrowed as did Nala's. They heard Whiz inside.

"Aye? What the fuck y'all shut the door for? Ain't shit in here, yo!"

Nala rushed up to the door and tried to open it, but it wouldn't budge. Tuck looked down at Kurt and saw a sadistic grin spreading across his face.

"Oh, shit! Aye! Sis! Tuck! Open the dooooorr!" Whiz began screaming.

Tuck ran to the digital padlock and tried entering the code again, but nothing happened. Kurt started cackling, as he continued bleeding out. Nala beat on the door, screaming for her brother, as sounds of what was like torches flaming up filled her ears.

"Open the dooooor! *Aaaaaggghhhh!*" Tuck and Nala heard Whiz cry.

Tuck pointed the gun at Kurt and snapped, demanding he give him the code to open the door. Kurt laughed.

"Fuck you… bitch ass…"

Boc!

"*Agh!*" Kurt screamed when Tuck fired once and shot him in his left kneecap.

"Gimme the code!" Tuck yelled.

"*Pleeeeaaase!*" Nala cried, hearing and smelling her little brother being roasted inside of what was thought to be a closet but was really an incinerator that Kurt used to destroy evidence linking his guilty clients to a crime.

Kurt gave them the finger, and through his pain, he laughed at them. Tuck roared angrily and emptied the rest of his clip into Kurt's face.

"*Calviiin*!" Nala cried her brother's real name out, as she beat on the door.

His screaming died down. Smoke billowed from under the door. What smelled like meat burning filled her nostrils.

Tuck, too stunned to move, stood stuck where he was. A few seconds later, Whiz's screams completely stopped.

"Goddammit!" Tuck cursed, while Nala cried her eyes out, still trying to get the door open.

He ran over to her and pulled her away. She tried to fight him off her.

"Nala! He's gone, yo! We can't stay! Come on!" he urged.

Knowing he was right, Nala relented and hurried off behind him. They flew up the stairs and out of the house to Nala's Range. Tuck got behind the wheel and then up out of there.

Nala started crying again, devastated over the horrible way her brother had just died. Tuck was furious, tired of losing. He had had it. His next move was going to be the one that brought Omar to him, and when he came, it was over for him.

Chapter 12

Kayla's wounds were cleaned, anti-bacterial ointment applied, then bandaged before getting dressed in a plain t-shirt and a pair of leggings. She felt a little better. The Percocet she took had her numb to the pain but not to how things could have just gone so very badly. She was beyond grateful that Omar came when he did, but she had to know how the hell did he just show up like that.

Kayla rubber banded her hair up in a messy bun, then barefoot, she left out of the spa-like bathroom, leaving heated marble flooring and stepping onto soft, beige carpet that was complemented by taupe walls trimmed with mahogany wood trim and ceiling beams. The guest bedroom Omar put her in was as grand as a master bedroom. Five-star luxury at its best, but Kayla's own house back in Pittsburgh was just as laid out. It had its own elevated balcony with weather resistant furniture for one to lounge and relax on with a view of the wilderness.

Exiting her room, Kayla checked on her girls. Chante, in a guest room of her own, was fast asleep after a strong concoction of tea, vodka, and Tylenol put her down. Jerrica was passed out, and Valerie was snoring her ass off. Silently thanking God that they were all still there, Kayla made her way down to the kitchen, craving a late-night snack.

***

In the refrigerator, Omar grabbed a pack of shredded turkey and dumped it into two separate bowls full of Blue Buffalo dry dog food, mixing it up real good. He set them down for Smoke and Haze, gave them fresh water, then let them fill up. He looked at Smoke, his Alpha male. He had cleaned the cut on his face and bandaged it. He didn't show any signs of pain, which Omar was grateful for.

Hearing footsteps right then, Omar looked toward the entryway of where his big, marble, stainless-steel and hardwood accented gourmet kitchen adjoined the spacious living room that was designed with high ceilings, rustic hardwood floors, Italian imported furniture, and a chic concrete fireplace with an eighty-inch HDTV built into it. He saw Kayla bend the corner and enter the kitchen in a t-shirt, leggings, barefoot, with her hair in a messy bun that made her look so fucking sexy to him. She saw him and seemed surprised. He looked at her and smiled.

"How you feel?" he asked her, leaning against the stainless French door Sub-Zero refrigerator.

Kayla looked up at him from where she had stopped in her tracks.

"I'm… cool. You?"

"Now that I know you and ya girlrillas are safe, I'm good."

"Is that right?" she asked, sounding sarcastic.

"Yeah, yo. Why you ask that, soundin' like I'm cappin'?"

"The question is why the fuck did you really just leave me hangin'?" Kayla snapped. "Them bitch ass niggaz was tryin' to kill me, O!"

"Kayla, I did not leave you hangin', girl! What in God's name would really make you think that?"

"Ya bitch! That's what!"

Omar's eyebrows furrowed. "My bitch? Who the… Aw, come on now, yo! Are you for real right now?"

"Yeah, nigga!"

Omar stepped toward her. Kayla stepped back and surprised him by balling her fists up.

"Oh, what? You gon' swing on me now?" he asked her, taking another step forward.

"If you walk up on me, I'ma splow you, yo! Homiez!" she told him.

He chuckled at her and kept approaching. She kept stepping back from him.

"O, stop! I'm mad at you right now, yo!"

"Why?"

"Because, nigga! You didn't come for me! I almost died! Some random ass dude rescued me! Why not you? My fuckin' homie!"

They lingered in the kitchen.

"Kayla, Claudia and I were enroute, yo. Some clown side swiped us purposely and sent us rollin' into someone's front yard. I woke up half a day later. I went to the BP you was callin' me from and paid the lil' snotty-ass bitch for the video of you to see how you left, so I could track you down. Chante called me before she could and told me to kick rocks basically."

Kayla laughed. "That's my girl!"

"Shut up, punk. How the hell you really gon' allow yaself to think I would abandon you, Kayla?"

Sighing, Kayla shrugged her shoulders.

"Man, you better answer my question, yo," Omar told her, closing the gap between them.

She looked into his eyes then. "How did you find us?"

"Well, when a nigga care about someone sooo much and somethin' happens to them, he loses his mind so much that it takes him a while to remember that his two $4,000 dogs have microchips implanted in them, and he has an app that gives him their location, which would lead me right to you. To me, it really looked like it was right on time that I showed up."

She went silent. Her head dropped down, shoulders slumping. Omar reached under her chin and tipped her head back up. He locked eyes with her, as she did with him. He could see so many emotions in her so close to coming out. His heartbeat sped up, as he began to feel something stir inside of him.

"Maybe," Kayla replied, voice softening some, as the anger in her eyes dissipated.

"Kayla," he called to her softly, voice deep and raspy.

She felt her nipples grow erect from the sensuous sound. Her temperature rose up like a thermometer dropped in a pot of boiling water.

"Yeah?" she replied, feeling unbelievably shy in front of him.

"Do you know how much I love you?"

A thousand butterflies tickled her from inside, and she couldn't stand still. Heatwaves shot through her core and headed south, turning into a tropical storm that started soaking her panties.

"I... love you too... O. You're my best friend."

"Naw, Kay. I do love you as my homie, my best friend, but I love you as way more."

He saw her eyes go wide.

"Wh-What do you... What are you sayin', Omar?" she nearly pleaded to know.

He took her hands into his, intertwining his fingers with hers. Looking down into her eyes, Omar broke it down for her.

"I'm in love wit you, Kayla. I have been for a really long time. I almost lost you... twice... all because of me."

"O, it's not..."

"Shhh! Lemme finish, Kayla," he cut her off. "Losin' you is the worst thing that could happen to me. I need you in my life, and I can't hold it in any longer. I want you as more than just my homegirl, baby. I want you as my woman. I wanna build a life wit' you, have kids wit' you. I wanna give you my heart, and I want yours in exchange."

Her eyes had filled with tears that spilled out and ran down her face. Omar used his thumbs to wipe them, then he cupped her beautiful face with his hands.

"Can I have it? Your heart?' he asked her, gazing down into her eyes.

Kayla took a few seconds before she was able to respond. She nodded her head then found the capability to speak.

"Yes. Just… don't break it."

"I won't. I promise," he swore, then he leaned down and pressed his lips to hers.

Kayla's eyes closed the second his lips touched hers. The blissful union of them coming together was as sweet and satisfying as homemade sweet potato pie. Her heart pounded in her chest. Nipples ached. Panties got wetter. She kissed him back. He matched her sudden aggressiveness, as she let go of all her reserve. Their kiss heated up, deepened, got wilder by the second. She moaned. He moaned. She panted. He panted. His hands took the bottom of her shirt and lifted it up. She broke from the kiss, so he could rid her of it. Her succulent 34-D cups, uncovered by a bra, made Omar's mouth water up. They were full, plump, nipples erect, looking like butterscotch Hershey's kisses.

He went for the waistline of her dark leggings. Careful not to disturb her injured leg, Omar rolled them down her thighs, exposing wet cotton panties. Getting them down to her ankles, Kayla stepped out of one leg then the other, then Omar took her saturated panties off.

"Damn, baby." He got a good look at the naked, tattooed work of art standing before him and marveled. "You are the epitome of gorgeous, Kayla. Homiez."

His words made her smile, while his admiring gaze made her feel like he had seen no woman more beautiful than her and never would.

"Your turn," she told him then bit her bottom lip in anticipation.

Omar grinned seductively at her. His t-shirt came off. Her eyes drank in perfectly chiseled body spiced with tattoos all over. He dropped his Nike basketball shorts, kicked out of them, then as she began dripping down her thighs, he dropped his boxers.

Kayla gasped at the sight of his ten-inch manhood, so thick and two-toned, pointing right at her. She took it into her hand, gripping it, giving it a gentle squeeze. Omar leaned in and kissed her again, picking up where he left off. Kayla moaned, temperature rising even higher. Then suddenly, she felt his hands sliding down her sides, down and around her juicy forty-six-inch ass. He cupped her cheeks and lifted her with ease, sitting her on the counter.

Omar's lips departed from hers and kissed along her jawline, down to her neck, as he stepped in between her legs. Kayla's back arched up from the feel of his soft lips on her flesh. They kissed downwards, from her neck to her chest. She nibbled on her lip when he lifted her right breast up and took her nipple into his mouth.

"Omar! Mmmm, shhit!"

He suckled her hungrily. Taking her left breast into his hand, he massaged it while continuing to suck her other nipple.

Kayla's toes curled and wiggled. She balanced herself on her hands, feeling like putty. Between her legs was so wet. Her clit, swollen, throbbing, yearned for him in the worst way.

Omar switched to her left breast and sucked her nipple. His hand traveled down her front, to between her legs, where her sweet spot was. He found her love button immediately and rubbed it while still sucking her breast.

The dual sensations Omar was giving her had Kayla ready to explode. She moaned his name, panted, then he kissed his way south, leaning her against the wall, opening her legs wide. The second Kayla felt Omar's lips on her, she threw her head back, eyes closed, back arched, and called out his name even louder.

Omar parted her, pushing the hood to her clit up, then put his lips to it. He sucked on it like making her climax was essential to life. He worked her, his lips and tongue making her go crazy. He snacked on her like she was perfectly made fried chicken dipped in sweet honey barbecue sauce.

"Omar! Ooo! Oh, shit! Oh, God, that feels so good, baby!" she cried out.

Grabbing her breasts, she started massaging them, adding more to her pleasure, while Omar munched.

He then slipped two fingers inside of her wetness. Curling them slightly, he stroked her G-spot while continuing to suck on her clit. Kayla went bananas. Her head spun around in circles like his tongue was doing.

A wave flowed around inside of her. She felt it trying to come out. She cried out seconds later, as it made her tremble then shake. Her back arched harder. Omar went crazier. Then, Kayla exploded in one gloriously intense orgasm that blew out of her like water from a whale's blowhole, all over Omar's face.

"Oh, my God! Holy shit!" she cursed, astounded by how her body felt like it was a live circuit of electricity, buzzing with satisfaction that she had not had enough of. "More, O! More!" she begged, panting hard, out of breath but still charged up.

Omar was ready to oblige her fervent request. He picked her up off the counter, carried her into the living room, and laid her on the fuzzy Alpaca fur rug by the fireplace. He got on top of her. She opened her legs and reached down, gripping his length. Omar felt his tip brush her slick, swollen lips. As she positioned him at her tunnel, he eased inside of her and was immediately overcome by the warm welcome she gave him.

"Aaaaeghhh, ssshhhit, baby! This pussy so good!" Omar groaned, feeling her tightness envelope him like she was made for him.

Kayla's eyes rolled to the back of her head. The bliss of him filling her up with the love she had craved since… forever… was so sweet that it made her lick her lips. He felt so delicious to her.

"Oooo, Omar!" she cried out. "Yeeesss! Shit! Mmmhmmm!"

"You like that, baby?" he asked in a low, husky tone that charged her up even more, while he stroked her slowly but with power.

"Yes, baby! Ooooohh, God, I fuckin' love it! Fuck me! Go hard, baby! Hit this pussy like you been wantin' to!"

He placed his hands on the sides of the floor by her head and went savage. He put power to the pussy, stroking it hard, pounding her like she begged for. He hit the bottom of the pussy hole and had her speaking in tongues. A few minutes later, Kayla exploded again.

Omar pulled out of her. He rolled onto his back and pulled her on top. Kayla slowly slid down on his dick, filling herself up with him. Grabbing his pecs, she started riding him, gyrating her hips. She looked down into his eyes, matching his gaze. She took it slow, getting used to sitting on a ten-inch dick when she hadn't gotten dicked down in a long time. The pain from his size stretching her out was worth it, as the pleasure came moments after. It made her want to sing.

"Yeah, baby! Goddamn! Ride this dick! Ride it like you *know* it's yours."

"Ooo, I am, Omar! And it *is* mine! All of it! It's mine!"

She turnt up on Omar then. Bouncing up and down on him, she fucked on his dick like there wouldn't be another chance. He reached up and grabbed her breasts, rubbing them, while she went up and down. She was so wet that the pussy farted over and over again. She drenched him but hadn't even cum yet.

124

"Kayla! Fuck! Goddammit! I love you, baby!"

"I l-love you, too, Omar! Oh, my God, I love you!"

She came all over him less than a minute later. Before she even had a chance to catch her breath, Omar had her on her left side and put himself on his right. He slid back in, holding her right leg up and murdered the pussy. Kayla cried and moaned into his chest, holding onto him for the wild ride. She couldn't help herself. She bit his right pec. Omar roared but didn't stop her. He welcomed the pain because it was love.

She climaxed again soon after. Omar flipped her onto her belly then pulled her hips up, making her toot that God Almighty ass up in the air for him. He got behind her and slid back in it. He wasted no time in going slow. He went ham, jackhammering her like she was a concrete sidewalk, and he was the tool to break her up. He looked down and marveled at her ass cheeks jiggling when his thighs slapped against hers.

"Ooooo, Omaaarr! Yeeesss! Ohh, Goood, fuck meee!" Kayla screamed, feeling an even more intense one coming on so strong that she started shaking like she had been stuck naked in a freezer for hours.

Omar felt his nut rising as well. He grabbed her ass and gave it all that he had. Right at the last moment, he put her back onto her back and stroke them both to oblivion, while they gazed into each other's eyes.

Kayla went limp with him still inside of her. She didn't want him to pull out. She wanted him to sleep in it.

Omar leaned down and kissed her lips softly, sensually. She kissed him back, arms wrapped around his neck. After a minute, Omar was on his back, Kayla's head on his chest. His arm pulled her all the way to him, then they both passed right out into deep, hot and spicy, sex comas.

Chapter 13

"I'm outside. Hurry up, yo," Tuck demanded.

"Here I come," replied Soulie and ended the call.

Tuck sat behind the wheel of his Challenger and waited. Parked in front of a house on Wheeler Street in Homewood, he waited for the dope man to emerge. Seconds after the call ended, Soulie, a super light-skinned guy with a tapered mini afro, came out and down the steps with a brown paper bag. He hopped in with Tuck and dapped him up.

"I'm glad to see you cool, cutty. I heard about what happened at ya store. Maan, what bitch got blown up behind it, yo?" Soulie asked him.

"Sheit, I have no clue. I wasn't even there," Tuck capped. "But check it. I got a deal for you."

"Okay? I'm listenin'."

"I told you ten gees for half a brick of the white. I'ma change that to $7,500. Move that, come back to me instead of that nigga, O, and you'll stay at a low price. How that sound?"

"Sounds like a deal to me, homie," Soulie agreed.

He pulled his cash out of the bag, took $2,500 out, and gave him the rest.

Tuck accepted the gwop and grabbed the half brick of cocaine he had under his seat that had come from Omar's homegirl's spot in East Liberty. He gave it to Soulie. Dapping him up, Soulie got out and ran back up the steps to his house.

Pulling off, Tuck rolled down Wheeler to Frankstown Avenue. Stopping at the stop sign, he peeped to his right and

126

saw his boarded-up store with police tape stretched across it. He was glad that the store wasn't in his name, but everyone knew it was his spot. Avoiding the cops because of the likelihood that he was wanted for questioning due to loose lips being paid to squeal, Tuck knew it was in his best interest.

Ahead of him, a barbershop with a graffiti painted front had a few young hood niggas standing on the corner by it. Tuck knew they were all Crips. Homewood was Crip City, well-known amongst those from the 4-1-2. Tuck also knew that the Criplets moved coke and heroin that came from big dogs that copped weight from Omar. There was a network of people moving dope and coke around Homewood, East Hills, Penn Hills, Monroeville, back down to Wilkinsburg, Larimer, East Liberty, Garfield, Bloomfield, the Northside, the Southside, and even the towns at the edge of Allegheny County into Westmoreland, and even parts of Ohio, New Jersey, Virginia, West Virginia, and Maryland.

Thinking about how widespread Omar had established himself to be made Tuck even more anxious to do better and shut Omar down. He truly hated Omar and wanted to see him die after he took everything from him. Memories of back when they were all young resurfaced in Tuck's head. They made him see red, like the blood he so badly wanted to see leak from Omar's lifeless body.

Tuck hit a left on Frankstown, ignoring the suspicious looks the Criplets were giving him, a few of them with their pistols upped and ready to pop at him. He shot up Frankstown, passing Blackadore and reaching where a Family Dollar sat at the tipped split of Frankstown Avenue, Bennett Street, and Tokay Street. He looped around, cutting a right on Bennett at the traffic light, then turned into the Family Dollar's lot.

He saw the older Pontiac Grand Prix by the rear corner, next to a dump truck that was parked. Pulling up to it, Tuck saw Rex behind the wheel, blazing a blunt.

Tuck rolled his window down and looked at Rex. The dark-skinned dreadhead produced a bookbag and tossed it through his window into Tuck's Challenger. Opening it, Tuck quickly counted five stacks of $10,000 rubber-banded bundles. Zipping the bag closed, he set it aside and got the brick of fentanyl-cut heroin, of which he put a special addictive in, from under his seat. He tossed it to Rex and watched the man examine it.

"You know you makin' too much noise out here, right?" Rex spoke, finally looking at Tuck, ashing his blunt out of his window.

"Good. That means niggaz is hearin' me. I'ma keep makin' noise too, cutty. This my hood, and I'ma always be in it."

Rex chuckled. "I hear ya. Be safe out here, cuz. It's been real wild. Niggas is getting spanked left and right."

At that, Rex rolled his window up, put the car in drive, and pulled off without another word.

"I'ma kill that nigga, yo. Homiez," Tuck told himself, recognizing a threat when he saw one.

He exited the parking lot and took Bennett past a trucking company with an auto repair/tow company across the street from it. Tuck was familiar with the people associated with the businesses in that particular ghetto part of Homewood. Dirty money came in, clean money came out, foot soldiers got paid, drug bosses relaxed in the sun with their families, sipping drinks out on the lanais of their lavish mansions. Tuck wanted that. After all the time he did in prison, keeping his mouth shut when he could have gotten so many people knocked and sent up the river, he felt owed. He wanted what was his, and he wanted it now.

Continuing down Bennett, he came to Oakwood and hit a left at the light. Cruising on, halfway up a curved hill, Tuck came to a small narrow side cut called Mulford and turned onto it. With Hamilton Avenue seconds up ahead of him, Tuck got ready to bust another right when red and blue lights suddenly began flashing behind him. The sirens blared for just a second then again, again, and again.

"Aight, pig, damn!" Tuck pulled over, annoyed by the cop playing with the siren then shining the bright spotlight on him, nearly blinding him.

Putting it in park, he took a deep breath and let it out. Leaning back in his seat, he waited for the cop to walk up. In his mirror, he saw the cop behind the wheel get out with a flashlight in hand. In his rearview mirror, he peeped another get out of the passenger's side. Shaking his head, Tuck chuckled to himself.

The tap on his window came seconds later. As he rolled the window down, the second cop tapped on the passenger's side. Groaning, he rolled it down as well.

"Don't y'all got anything better to do tonight than pull a Black man over a week away from Juneteenth?"

He looked to his left and up at her right as Amber started laughing.

With the spotlight still on, Tuck could see her shapely figure perfectly. Even in plain clothes consisting of a tie-dye t-shirt, skinny-leg jeans, Nike's, and her bulletproof vest, she was still a sexy-ass white bitch. Tuck wanted to fuck her so badly, but Amber acted like she didn't like dick… her partner though on the other hand. Tuck looked over at Cammie. She was also in plain clothes with a vest on, slightly slimmer than her brunette partner with her sandy-brown hair pulled back in a tight bun. Tuck saw her smile at him. It was the same smile that she put on before someone died.

"Well, we've been meaning to talk to you, ya know? Give our condolences about your store and to whoever got blown up behind it," Amber told him. "Plus, Ace has been handled."

Tuck nodded. "Good. What about Omar?"

"You seem to have a real problem with him. Why exactly?" asked Amber.

He refused to tell her.

"Look, I just want his ass gone. When will it happen?"

"When we have $250,000 paid in full," he heard Cammie interject.

"What? A quarter million? For that bitch ass nigga?"

"Yup. You see, that bitch ass nigga has been who you have wanted gone for a long time. He had a lot of friends and a lot of money. A big target like that, you are gonna have to pay big."

"Or!" came Cammie again. "We can reach out to Omar, tell him what you've been up to, and I'd bet every dime I've made off of your ass that he'd easily fork over the money to have us wipe *you* out."

"Wow. Well, gimme the shit y'all got from Ace's spot and I got you."

Amber laughed. "Nuh uh. That's ours. Finder's fee we'll call it."

"What's it gonna be, Mr. Holloway?" Amber asked, addressing Tuck by his last name. "Time is money, and yours is in question."

"Okay. Two hunnid fitty it is. I need to get back to you though," he told Amber. "Money doesn't just grow on trees, yah mean?"

She chuckled. "Sure doesn't, which is why…"

Pausing mid-sentence, she dug into one of the pockets of her vest and pulled out a piece of paper, folded it up, and handed it to him.

"I'll make getting your money up easy. That is a grocery list of spots that are holding big time. Lots of firepower in 'em though, so I suggest going with someone you trust who isn't afraid to get bloody. The rules are make sure that I know before you go shopping, so I can keep you clear 'til you leave the store. Cammie and I get half of everything, and don't get cute ideas, trying to skim us. We'll know."

"And we'll be very upset with you, Tuck," Cammie added with a smile so ominous that Tuck wanted to throw Holy water in her face.

"I'll expect a call from you soon, Tuck. Take care. Oh. One last thing," Amber remembered. "Click it or ticket. Seat belts save lives, so buckle up... no pun intended."

The crooked hit-cops took their leave then. Hopping back into their unmarked Impala, they pulled off, going around Tuck and swerving down Hamilton.

Tuck stayed where he was for another minute, refusing to move until he was sure they were gone, so they wouldn't follow him to his next drop. Looking at the paper, Tuck unfolded it and looked at the list.

"Oh, word!" He saw a few names on the list that he'd been planning to hit up, and they were indeed holding. "Period. On the Homiez, I'm in there, and I need all of that."

Putting the paper in his pocket, Tuck put his car in drive. As he pulled off, he got out his phone and made a call that was answered as he made a right turn down Hamilton.

"Yeah?" Nala asked, sounding like she had been sleep.

"I got somethin' for us to do. I'ma be another hour but be ready by then. You gon' love this, yo."

"Mhmm. Bye."

The call ended as Tuck got to the bottom of the hill. Grinning widely at the visions of the come ups, he hit a left turn onto Rosedale and cruised on, putting it all together in his head so that no matter what, there would be no failures.

***

Giggling and soft chatter awakened Kayla late the next morning. Her eyes flicked open. Bright sunlight was in her face. Stinging sensations immediately pinged in her leg, and her head wound ached.

"Shhhh! See! Y'all woke her up, yo! Run!"

Hearing feet making a dash for it, Kayla shifted and just caught a glimpse of Chante, Jerrica, and Valerie bending the corner to the kitchen with Smoke and Haze right behind them. Kayla shook her head then regretted it when it felt like her brain ripped loose from her spine.

"Ow," she whimpered, closing her eyes again.

"Hey."

His voice, soft and velvety smooth, made her open her eyes, feeling brave enough to face the light if it meant that she could see the handsome dope man's face. Kayla looked at Omar. He sat up next to her, looking her in her eyes. His fresh gaze made her feel so shy that she wanted to hide, but there wasn't anywhere that she could go fast enough.

"You okay?" he asked her.

"My head… my leg… I'm good. You?"

"Beside knowin' that I can't carry the pain you feel, I'm very good."

Kayla's lips curled into a huge, bashful smile. Omar leaned toward her and kissed her lips. Her yes closed. She focused on how he felt, how he smelled, more than how he looked… ass naked, like she was, on an expensive area rug. Only after he pulled back did she open her eyes. He smiled. She smiled back.

"I enjoyed it. More than ever before," Omar told her.

"Mhmm. Sure."

"I'm dead ass serious. I wouldn't cap about that."

Kayla giggled. It surprised her that she could even do that.

"Well, just so you know… Uh, we're busted, bae."

"Busted?" he questioned.

"Chante, Jerrica, Valerie, Smoke and Haze, all was just in here and saw us… like this."

"Like this? Oohhh… you mean like *this?*" Omar rolled on top of her, catching her by surprise.

Kayla squealed, laughing her ass off, as Omar kissed all over her.

"Omar, baby, stooop, they're gonna seeee!" she playfully whined, though she in no way wanted him to stop.

"And? Let 'em see. Let 'em see how much I love you and ain't afraid to show it."

Kayla let out a sigh, one of contentment, happy to be where she was. She kissed him again. His lips and his warm body made her forget about her head and leg. He was relieving her pain just by being on top of her, kissing her, loving her, and cherishing her. Never before had she felt so cared for and wanted, especially by someone she cared for and that she wanted.

"I love you too, O," she told him.

Omar reached over for his phone then. It had died some time after he had used the dogs' microchip app to track Kayla down.

"I need to charge my phone. How about we shower, I cook for us all, then you and ya' girls can take one of my whips and go get y'all some clothes 'n shit?"

"You had me at cookin' for us then lost me at the part where you wanna get rid of me."

"What?" Omar's eyebrows furrowed.

"Yeah, nigga. I said it." Kayla narrowed her eyes at him, scowling.

"Knock it off, Kayla. You wanna stay in the same clothes, then be my guest. I didn't exactly expect to be comin' here, so there's no bunches of gifts for you like there was before. Plus, I'm sure you ain't got cash on you or ya bank cards."

She looked at him.

"And what exactly are you gonna do if I say I'll go, Omar?"

"Figure out how I'ma get them couches back home, check in on my niggaz, then my businesses. Pretty much stay here wit' Smoke and Haze while I do that."

Kayla let out another sigh.

"Okay. I'ma trust you. We need to go get Jerrica's whip from the motel I was at anyways."

"Aye, who was this dude that rescued you?"

"He goes by Beast. His ass is nuts, yo. Got screws loose or somethin'. When we snatched up ol' boy and put him in the trunk, Beast was supposed to get up wit' us, but he just disappeared. Then, we got rear ended, cops almost got us, then you came."

"Hold up… You had a nigga in the trunk of the car that I blew up?"

"Yeah. The one that ran this… mob. I guess they are called EBK, which is who came after me when I went to get food."

"Oh, word? Well, fuck that nigga then."

"Naw, O. Not fuck him. I wanted answers. Someone put him on us. I would've made him tell us."

Omar paused to think about it. Someone put a mob leader on Kayla, who was not known in Wisconsin, and therefore couldn't be a target. He surmised that it had to be an attempt on him since he was the one that came to drop bricks off and take money back. He told this to Kayla and saw her eyes spark like a forest that had a tropical storm of gasoline poured all over it then a match lit and tossed in.

"There's a list of people that are competition with Claudia, but there's only one muhfucka I can think of that would go that far. I need to put my phone on charge and call her, bae. If it's who I think, I'm gonna go find dude and dead that bitch ass nigga."

"Who?" Kayla asked.

"Claudia's baby daddy, Jerrod."

Kayla shook her head with disdain just at the sound of her name. Adding fuel to the fire that burned inside of her for Claudia, a nigga that the bitch has a child with coming after *her* had Kayla's mind instantly filled with thoughts of Claudia trying to set *her* nigga up.

Not happenin'. On my muthafuckin' dead Homiez, yo. If that bitch comes near my man again, she gon' come up missin'. And it's a wrap for her baby daddy whenever I catch his ass…

"The enemy of my nigga is my enemy, baby. I'm ready. We can go…"

"No, Kayla." Omar cut her right off. "You have been shot, been in two crashes, and almost arrested, all because of me. I…"

"Omar, lemme…"

"Kayla! No! I need you to chill! You are wounded! Ya head is cracked, and you got bullet holes in ya leg! I am beggin' you to let me handle it!"

Kayla looked him right in his eyes. She wanted to protest. To tell him that she wasn't a baby nor was she out of the game because of a wound. But one thing she knew was that a man, especially one like Omar, was a natural protector. He had to protect. It was deep seeded in his divine ancestry as a Black man to keep what was his safe from harm.

As much as she wanted to be that girlrilla that everyone knew she was, Kayla surmised that now with her newfound… status… she could fall back a little and let the man do what he felt was needed. Besides, she knew if help was needed, she would be the first one that he called.

"Okay, Omar. Relax, yo."

Omar reached for her and pulled her closer. He kissed her forehead and then leaned his against hers.

"Thank you, Kay. I promise you everything will get taken care of. You gotta remember though. I did just murk a group of cops. I guarantee that there's a manhunt goin' on that I gotta make sure I never get put into."

"We," Kayla corrected.

"How is it we?" he asked her.

"When we snatched dude up, I let Smoke and Haze get at the cop that was about to arrest him. Him gone."

Omar couldn't help but chuckle at her.

"Maan, you's a crazy woman, yo. Come on and let's go shower. I'ma clean you up real good, while I try to keep my hands to myself."

"And if you do that, then my hands will *force* yours to do what you know they wanna do. So, take me to your shower and handle that business before our day starts. Now, nigga."

All too eager to oblige and dive deep up in that wet-wet again, Omar jumped up, ass naked, dick swinging, and scooped Kayla up in his arms.

"Well, damn! Okay, then, Mr. Strong Nigga!" she laughed.

"You make me strong, baby," he told her sincerely, then without waiting another minute, Omar took off for his bedroom to get to his marble spa master bathroom, so he could relieve more of her pain before they started their day.

Chapter 14

Ice burst out laughing hard at the price his nephew had just told him. Jerrod, not amused, looked at the 6'4", super bright skinned, old school pimp nigga in a pink Gucci button up shirt, Gucci slacks, and Gucci loafers on his feet. The gold chains around his neck shined like the Rolex on his wrist, the rings on his fingers, the gold in his mouth, both ears, and the frames of his Gucci shades. His long, brown hair was laid back from the perm he had in it. His pencil-thin mustache and goatee were razor sharp and trimmed.

At his sides in the royal purple, gold, and hardwood trimmed living room of his house on 19th and Avers in Chicago's *Holy City* section were two bad ass chicks in tiny dresses, heels, hair and makeup done, nails did, and dripping in gold jewelry as well. One was as black as an African while the other, a redbone.

The two burst out laughing with Ice at Jerrod, and it burned him up even more to have sluts in the mix.

"Aw, man! Aye, nephew, you a funny guy, joe. Ain't nobody payin' pandemic prices anymore, man. Ya got 'ta come betta than thirty-five grand for a brick of dope."

Jerrod shook his head. "Unc, this shit is raw. I had a tooter and a shooter try the shit, and they told me they ain't ever had dope that good."

"Hmmmm." Ice rubbed his chin and thought for a second. "They said that, huh? That's rare. Cluck don't eva say dope is top notch because they know you'll tax, and that's bad for them."

Ice was a player, born and raised out Chicago's west side. He was a Conservative Vicelord, a 5-Star Universal Elite, and had been in the game for forty-five years, starting out at just ten years of age. Jerrod knew his uncle had been the man to see if one wanted to make moves in the Holy City. Though he had been born and raised in Kenosha, he had frequented Chicago to visit family whenever his mother took him there. His favorite relative, though, was Ice. The man had always been the shit to Jerrod. He had money, girls, cars, designer clothes, and was a real-life gangster.

After hitting Knuck's spot up for the merch, Jerrod called his uncle up, told him what was up, and got an invite to slide through. Geeked, Jerrod was sure that he would turn his come-up into cash, then that cash would get him some *payow – that good shit –* and he could start his rise.

"See what I'm sayin', Unc. Why is that price bad?" Jerrod asked him.

"Because niggas out here in Chicago will rob yo' ass if you try to move dope in these streets wit' too high a tax. And you ain't even from here, 'Rod. Come on now, lil nigga. Use yo' head. This is Chiraq, not Keno."

The ladies laughed again. Jerrod wanted to smack them. Ice held his hand up, and they went silent.

"Charla, Alexus. Please excuse us for a minute."

The black beauty and light and lovely obediently took their leave, heading for the kitchen. When they were gone, Jerrod felt a little more at ease.

"Don't mind those two. They dick-ride for a livin'." Ice chuckled, while Jerrod didn't. "So, tell me. How's yo' son and that pretty girl you had him with?"

"My son good. Saw him yesterday,' Jerrod capped. "And fuck his mama. She left a nigga hangin' when I got locked up."

Ice shook his head. "You youngstas kill me wit' that 'it ain't my fault' shit."

Jerrod went to defend himself, but the moment he opened his mouth, Ice held his hand up, silencing him.

"Don't interrupt me, Jerrod. I'm gon' learn you somethin' that those lil dumb ass niggas out in these streets didn't learn. It *is* yo' fault! You got sent to prison cause you felt the need to rob an opp. Yo' baby mama got a bag! You disrespected her by cheatin' on her and callin' her outta her name, yet she brought yo' son into the world. By my code, when a woman becomes the motha of yo' child, ya dig what I'm sayin', she is nothin' less than a woman. She ain't yo' bitch or yo' ho. Yo' child breathes because of her! Show that girl some respect cause I don't think you could push a baby outta yo' ass afta dealin' wit' a knucklehead nigga like you the whole pregnancy!"

Jerrod was on the verge of blowing up on his uncle, but he knew Ice was not a chump. Plus, he needed his help.

"Aight, Unc. You right. Now, can you help me or what?"

"Yeah. I know what to do. We gon' buss them thangz down 'n hit 'em up good and double them joints. We gon' turn the deuce to a fo' and re-up and do it again, but ya gots to be patient and smart. Drug dealas and gangstas don't live full lives in Chicago."

"You have," Jerrod spoke with a raised eyebrow.

"I don't sell drugs, and I ain't no gangsta, youngin'. I sell pussy, and I'm a muthafuckin' Viceloooord!" Ice represented, throwing up VL with his right hand, grinning widely.

EBK, nigga. Yo' old ass can get it if you don't help me, Jerrod maliciously thought while smiling back at his uncle.

"So, we on then?" he asked.

"Yeah, 'Rod. I got everything we gon' need here." Ice stood up from his big leather chair then. "Bring ya ass. We got some work to do then some people to see."

Jerrod got up and followed his uncle, hoping to God that coming to Chicago with his stolen dope was a good move. If it was, then he would try to pop off the diamond jewelry he had swiped, the guns for some that he knew were clean, then take all that money and get even more dope. Or… he would rob someone else that he knew that wouldn't see it coming until he put a bullet in their eye.

***

The hot water raining down on them from the rain-down style shower ceiling only added to the blazing hot marble and glass enclosed shower. The glass and the windows were fogged all the way up. The sensational pleasure Kayla was feeling from Omar's tongue had her so hot that she felt like, at any moment, she would spontaneously combust. Her hands were against the wall, and leaning forward, ass poked out, she could barely contain herself, as Omar ate her ass.

His face was buried in her crack. His tongue slurped and licked all up and down her crevice, teasing her asshole, then he stuck it inside of her. Kayla squealed in delight, raising up on her tiptoes, trying to squeeze the veined marble tiles with her hands to attempt to combat the mind-blowing pleasure that had her going crazy.

A minute later, Omar pulled his face out and stood, dick throbbing, hard as hell, ready to dive into her again, but Kayla stopped him after he turned her to face him. Looking up at him, she wrapped her hand around his length. She saw it in his eyes. He wanted it. She slid down to her knees, ready to give it. Holding him in her hand, Kayla put her lips to it and kissed the bulbous tip. She opened her mouth while gripping him at the base and took him into her mouth, slowly engulfing him inch by inch.

Omar's eyes rolled to the back of his head. The shower was hot, but her oral skills were hotter. Kayla took him all the way in, surprising herself in the process. She'd given a few guys the pussy in the past, let a few hit from the back, but she had never allowed any of them to fuck her in the ass, nor had she ever sucked a dick before. To her, those two things should be kept for one that she would easily let all the way loose with, one that she knew would appreciate how sexual she could be and allow her to be open without ever questioning her about if she had done that with another nigga and how many.

Omar was that one – the one she could feel free with and feel no shame in pleasing her man. She had no problem giving him all of her because he was giving her all of him. Kayla cupped his balls with her left hand and gripped his shaft with her right. She massaged him, jerked him, and sucked him all at the same time. Omar's head felt like it was going to explode. He couldn't take it any longer.

He took his dick from her mouth and pulled her up from the floor. Roughly, Omar put her up against the wall. Kayla opened up for him and allowed him to enter. He eased in and held her up, while he beat it up. She wrapped her arms around his neck and held on for the ride. Her legs wrapped around him, squeezing him, while he pounded her, filling her with euphoric bliss with every stroke.

"Omar! Baby! Fuuuck, I'm gonna cum!"

"Me too, baby! Shit!"

A minute later, they both climaxed at the same time while gazing into each other's eyes. Their hearts pounded, chests rising and falling rapidly, as they breathed heavily with each other.

"Why the fuck did it take you so goddamn long, O?" Kayla suddenly asked, scowling at him like an angry bird.

It was so random and funny that Omar burst out laughing. He couldn't for the life of him hold it in. Kayla started laughing because of him.

"My fault, baby," Omar said, calming himself. "I never spoke of my feelings cause relationships fail, and friendships can be destroyed. You mean the world to me, Kayla. I can't stand the thought of losin' you for any reason."

"You're not gonna lose me, O. Do you love me?"

"Hell yeah! I do!"

"And I love you. This is real love, the kind that's been around forever, building up, getting stronger. Now that's it's bein' acknowledged, we can't be separated nor broken. We too strong for that, bae."

Omar let her down, setting her on her feet. He kissed her lips, cupping her face with his hands, then smiled.

"We are," he agreed." I got you; you got me. That's it; that's all."

Kayla smiled back.

"Kay-O, baby," she then said, bringing up their combined name their people gave them.

Omar chuckled.

"Kay-O, love. Kay muthafuckin' O."

***

After she took Omar's braids out, they both washed and conditioned each other's hair, then they washed each other's bodies, rinsed, and got out to dry, moisturize, and deodorize. Kayla dried his hair and combed it back into a big puff ponytail, then she pulled her own hair into a bun on top of her head.

Smoke and Haze were on Omar's bed when they came out of the room, laid out, basking in the sunlight that shone down from the skylight in the ceiling.

Omar bandaged Kayla's leg and thigh then applied liquid Band-Aid to the gash on her head. He helped her get dressed in the t-shirt and leggings she'd had on with her Jordans. Giving her his bank card, the pin number, and a Gucci bag full of rubber banded big faces, he put on a pair of boxers, basketball shorts, and a tank top before they headed out of the bedroom to the kitchen.

***

Chante, Jerrica, and Valerie were in the kitchen when Kayla and Omar and the dogs came down. The three snickered to themselves, which earned them all the middle finger from Kayla. Omar scrambled up some eggs, made turkey bacon, and toasted bread for everyone, pouring fresh orange juice. He ate with the ladies after he gave his dogs food and fresh water. Once they were done, they all headed outside to Omar's four car garage.

"Where's the SUV you brought us here in?" Kayla asked, noticing it wasn't where Omar parked it, and he had not left her side since they got there.

"It went to join the Titanic," Omar told her, handing the key fob with *Dodge* on it to her. "Made a call once we got here for it to be taken away."

"Oh… and we're all clear?" she asked.

"No suspects but cops and Feds searchin'," Chante cut in, holding up her phone with a natural news feed on the screen, informing the public of five murdered Kenosha Police officers, one likely mauled by a dog, the others shot to death by an assault rifle, but absolutely no suspects known.

"Those dudes at the house we was at though," Chante added. "It look like the investigation gon' be on them and only them."

"Nothin' links y'all or me to the murders," Omar added in. "Just don't do nothin' else but go get cha' shop on and come back."

He hit the button on the remote opener for the garage. Door number two opened, revealing a shiny, black, 2023 Hellcat Dodge Durango on blacked-out SRT wheels.

"Gurnee Mills Mall is eight minutes away from here. The stores are aight. Enough to at least get fresh. It's programmed in the navigation and just know this SUV is very safe."

He pulled Kayla to him, then he kissed her breath away. When he let her go, she turned toward her girlrillas and saw them all grinning their asses off at her.

"Y'all will be walkin' if any of y'all say anything. On the Homiez," she promised and headed toward the driver's door to get in.

"Byyyyee, Omar!" the three sang out, goofy as hell, before hopping into the Hellcat truck with Kayla.

The engine spit powerfully to life when Kayla started it. Omar waited for her to pull out of the garage. He blew a kiss to her, though he couldn't see her or the others through the dark tints. Kayla beeped, then at the end of the driveway, she made a turn, following the GPS announcer's directions. Omar looked down at Smoke and Haze then.

"Well, let's go back inside, shall we? I know people been tryna call me like crazy, especially Claudia," he told them, then heading back inside, he went back to his bedroom, got his phone, and turned it on.

***

Charla turned the special 1998 Mulliner Bentley Arnage Turbo RT into the vacant lot on 16th and Drake. Inside, a few old schools with custom paint jobs and decked out interiors were sitting on big rims, parked in a row. A group of young niggas and some females were out there kicking it, enjoying the weather. Charla bypassed them and rolled Ice's Bentley toward the three foreigns parked near the rear.

An all-red Rolls Royce Cullinan Black Badge on red Forgiatos sat next to a gold Lamborghini Urus sitting on black Forgiatos that matched its black racing stripes, and in front of both of them was a brand new extended wheelbase Rolls Royce Phantom on white Forgiatos. Pulling up close to the Phantom, Jerrod saw a muscular man by the big land yacht standing with a beautiful woman and two other men that were also accompanied by a woman of their own.

Charla and Alexus got out of the RT's front. They opened the doors for Ice and Jerrod. The two got out and walked up to the dark-skinned, muscled guy with long wicked dreadlocks. He was sporting a Chrome Hearts fit with special Chicago-edition Air Jordan 1s on his feet and was flossing diamond-encrusted jewelry like he owned a diamond store.

Jerrod noticed the two other guys, one golden-brown toned, tall, muscular, with a clean-shaven head and beard, rocking Hellstar and special edition Retro 5 Mikes, the other with a bald-fade, low beard, average height and slim, with cocoa-brown skin, swagged out in Amiri. Their ladies were model-type chicks, black beauty epitomized in designer dresses and heels with their hair, nails, and light makeup on point.

Walking up to them, Jerrod saw his uncle shake hands with the three men. Then, he spoke instructions.

"Jerrod, these brothas have been good friends of mine for as long as I can remember. The brotha wit' those long, crazy dreads, he goes by Chino, and the tall, Debo lookin' nigga is Shotgun."

The three men and their ladies all chuckled at Ice.

"And last, that's KoKo."

"KoKo?" questioned Jerrod.

"Yeah," Chino spoke up. "Cause his ass crazy like a coo-coo bird."

They all laughed again.

"My brothas, this is my nephew, Jerrod. He's from Kenosha but gots a few of us down hea'. He'd like to request permission to move a lil' dope out here and get some money."

"Yeah?" Chino looked at him. "You a Vicelord?"

"Naw. I don't gangbang," Jerrod capped.

Chino nodded.

"Why you can't sell yo' dope in Kenosha?" asked Shotgun with a suspicion expression etched in his face.

Just before Jerrod could answer, heavy bass shook the ground, loud air filling the air. They all looked toward the lot's entryway and saw a gleaming blue Hummer H2 SUT pickup on twenty-six-inch chrome rims pulling in.

The young Vicelords immediately grabbed AK-47 pistols and stood in the Hummer's path, pointing at the windshield. Jerrod went for the Glock in his waistline.

"Relax, nephew. It's cool," Ice told him.

They all saw a bald, dark-skinned guy's head come out of the window. With a very raspy voice, he started snapping.

"Aye, man! Get cha'll lil asses up outta my way! I'll run y'all ova! This bitch bulletproof!"

Jerrod heard Ice and the others laughing.

"Let dude through, joe!" Chino hollered to the young Lords.

Watching them fall back, Jerrod's eyebrows furrowed. The driver of the Hummer hit the gas and shot over toward where he and the O.G. Vicelords stood. Hitting the brakes, putting it into park, the driver, one that was definitely an ol' school cat, hopped out in a black t-shirt, Balmain jean shorts, with fresh black and blue Jordan 12s on his feet. Hopping out of the front seat was a heavyset dude with a headful of tiny dreads, a chin with pointed hairs, and a mustache. He rocked a Ralph Lauren polo, cargo shorts, and clean Air Forces on his feet, and he had gold-framed tinted Versace shades on.

"Aye! Whaz happenin', goddammit?! I say goddammit whaz happenin'?!"

Jerrod looked at the O.G. as he dapped Ice up then Chino, Shotgun, and last, KoKo.

"Who dis nigga right hea'? He don't look familiar," the loud, raspy man asked, looking at Jerrod.

Ice stepped up to him, towering over the 5'9" tall guy by at least a half a foot.

"This my nephew, Rob. Don't be slidin' up in hea' ridin' all crazy like that again. Keep that shit ova thea' on the otha' side of Pulaski, joe."

Ice then turned to Jerrod and introduced him to the O.G.

"Nephew, this is Rob G. He one of them K-town niggas wit' his GD ass."

Chino, Shotgun, and KoKo burst out laughing as did their ladies.

"Aye, man! Watch yo muthafuckin' mouth, Vicelord! I'll have all my lil youngins cross over and paint the Holy City blue!" Rob G threatened.

Jerrod peeped the fat dude's hand moving toward his waist. In a flash, Jerrod upped his .40 and pointed it at the guy's face.

"Try it, my nigga! I'll blow yo' bitch ass down right hea'!" he swore then cocked it.

The guy's hand fell to his side, eyes cutting toward Jerrod behind his tinted lenses. Ice, Rob G, Chino, Shotgun, and KoKo all looked toward Jerrod and Rob's people.

"DY? Fuck yo' ass doin', nigga?" he asked.

"I ain't on shit," DY replied, still staring at Jerrod's pistol.

"Nephew, relax. Rob is a friend, and DY is just a little ova protective," Ice spoke up.

"Dude's hand went toward his waist, like he's finna up the banger on you, Unc," Jerrod told Ice, lowering his gun to his side.

"Naw, lil nigga. DY ain't that stupid," Rob G told him then looked at DY, scowling at him. "He know muhfuckas are at peace 'round hea'. Ain't that right, DY?"

DY nodded. "Yeah."

"Good. Go'n 'n get back in the truck. I'll be thea' in a minute."

Obediently, DY did as told. Jerrod almost burst out laughing when he saw the man had a bald spot at the back of his head, which now made his dreads look like a bird's nest.

"That nigga needs to cut that shit, man." Rob G laughed as DY got back in the passenger's seat. "Whoever brought his ass home to the Fo' Corner Hustlas needs a new job. His ass crazy, joe."

"Aye, Rob, what chu' need? We's havin' a meetin' befor' you pulled up," Chino told him.

"Oh, my bad. I's just tryna let cha'll niggas know that I got a few pounds of that fi' y'all be wantin'."

"Aight, cool, joe. Muhfucka hit cho' line later," Ice told him, dismissing him.

Rob G started grinning.

"Yup. Hit me up when y'all get done wit' y'all meetin'." He looked at Jerrod. "See you around, lil nigga."

Jerrod waited until Rob G was back up in his Hummer then about facing and exiting the lot before he tucked his gun.

"Anyways," Ice continued, getting Jerrod's attention but addressing Shotgun's question. "My nephew brought his dope to me because he hit a lick on a Kenosha based group of them lil niggas that call themselves EBK."

"I heard of them," KoKo spoke up. "They on some bar none, renegade shit. They be on it, but they bleed like 'erybody else."

"They bet' not come through hea' screamin' that shit,' Shotgun added.

"Aight, joe," Chino spoke then, looking at Jerrod. "I'ma go'n 'n let chu get chu some money, Jerrod. Don't put no poison in that shit and have niggas and bitches droppin' dead on my streets. We don't need no muhfuckin' Hank Voights comin' 'round this bitch tryna get to startin' shit. Ya' dig I'm sayin', joe?"

Jerrod nodded. "Yes, sir."

"Okay, then. Oh, and one last thing," Chino got ready to add. "Do *not* go across Pulaski, joe. 16th and Pulaski is the border. Our hood is not exactly cool wit' K-town, so stay in the Holy City, and you'll be good."

"Aight," Jerrod agreed.

Ice then whistled for Charla and Alexus. They opened the rear doors to his Bentley and stood by. Thanking the three Ghosts for their time, Ice and Jerrod went and got back into the RT. The ladies closed the doors, got in front, then Charla pulled off.

"So, when do I start, Unc?" Jerrod asked Ice, as Charla turned out onto 16th.

"Now. We finna go over to Lawndale. I got a few young brothas that can help out. You ain't known 'round hea', so you gon' need the assistance of those that are, so clucks won't think you twelve or a shiester."

Nodding his head, Jerrod said nothing more but started thinking about his baby momma, getting his revenge, taking his son, and becoming the man in Kenosha to see for coke, dope, weed, guns, and girls after he shut down everyone else that thought they were plugged but were really mules.

Chapter 15

Red. Hot. Fury. Omar grinded his teeth together, as his blood boiled like lava soon to erupt. Seeing the frantic texts from all of his people in Pittsburgh about Ace and Kurt had him ready to hop on a plane and go blam on everyone that he had beef with. But he knew that would be pointless. He knew exactly who was responsible for it.

"I swear to God, yo! I'm gonna chop pieces off of that clown-ass nigga while he's alive until he dies!" Omar growled.

Smoke and Haze sat in front of him, as if they were ready to put some work in. Omar closed his eyes and spoke to the Man above, asking Him to take care of Ace, Shatonya, Kurt, and his wife, Francesca, and to forgive him in advance for the hell on Earth he was going to bring when he got back to the Steel City.

He checked on Kayla. She and the girlrillas sounded like they were having a good time. He chose not to ruin it by telling her about Ace just yet. He was surprised that she didn't already know. She and her homegirls were just as respected and known in the streets as he was.

After he checked on a few of his legit businesses – a charter bus company, a parking warehouse, a pet supply store, and a corner store – Omar's phone rang. He saw Claudia's name on the screen and answered her call.

"What up?"

"Someone broke into my house and stole my Rubicon."

"Get the fuck outta here."

"I'm for real. I just actually discovered it this morning when I went to get the key to take it to come see you."

"Don't you got cameras in ya crib?" Omar asked, swearing that she once told him about motion-capturing interior cameras.

"Yep, and that dumb muthafucker just made it to the top of my shit list."

"Lemme guess, Jerrod."

"Bingo. Come open the door. I dropped my son off at my mother's house, and I brought Hennessy and Tesla to see Smoke and Haze."

"Be right there."

Omar got up and made his way to the front door. When he opened it, along with the fresh breeze that flowed in, her sweet perfume wafted into his nostrils.

Her two female Blue Bloods went wild with excitement when Smoke and Haze ran out to them. The bigger of the two was Hennessy, and her sister, Tesla, was silent and wickedly fast. They were almost as big as Smoke and Haze and had clipped ears, muscular frames, and they had solid steel-blue fur. Omar had wanted them to mate, so he could train the pups, and then, he and Claudia could check a big bag off of them. He also had plans to gift Kayla with a pup of her own.

At that moment, all that left Omar's mind. All he could focus on now was the breathtaking, sexy Albanian belle that stood at his door dressed like she had rolled out of bed with dick on her mind.

Her hair looked wet, like she had just gotten out of the shower. She had black eyeliner and glossy red on her lips. She had on a little, red Valentino dress with a neck strap, open back, and a flared, mid-thigh hem that allowed her freshly waxed and oiled legs to be on full display. On her feet were red, pointed-toe pumps with gold chains as ankle straps and gold, six-inch heels that matched the Valentino earrings in her ears, the necklaces around her neck, and the

Audemars Piguet on her wrist. Her nails were also done, painted red to match her dress, with white stars airbrushed on them.

"You must got a date or somethin'," Omar said to her, unable to not ogle Claudia.

She smiled. "No, but I'll take that to mean that you like what you see, as I imagined you would."

Claudia stepped into his house then. Omar stood at the door for a minute. The dogs were running around, going crazy in the expansive front yard with each other. He closed the door, knowing he didn't need to watch them or worry about wild animals that likely needed to worry about *them* if they intruded on Smoke's and Haze's territory.

Claudia had gone into the kitchen and got a bottle of Pinot Grigio from the champagne chiller. Omar entered as she was pouring two flutes of the soothing liquid. She picked one up and held it for Omar.

"It's just about to be one in the afternoon, Claudia."

"And? I think you and I have earned the right to sip whenever we want, and you look just as stressed as I am. So, drink."

Omar grabbed the flute and sipped it. Claudia sipped hers, then she looked at him, licking remnants of the Pinot from her lips in the most enticing way.

"Where's yo' homegirl at?" She wanted to know, as she ran a finger around the rim of her glass.

"Shoppin' wit' her friends. Tell me more about this bitch ass nigga breakin' into ya crib and peelin' off in ya whip."

Claudia took another sip of her bubbly then set it down. Looking at him with her big, bright, blue eyes, she started toward him with a seductive walk that was amped by the sound of her sexy, red, high heels.

"Fuck Jerrod. I do not want to talk about him," she told Omar, coming to stop right in front of him. "I don't want to talk at all. I want you in the worst way, Omar."

She grabbed him by his tank top and yanked him down to her for a kiss, but he pulled back.

"Claudia, I can't. Kayla is my woman now. I can't do her like that, especially after all she's went through because of me."

Claudia looked at him. Nodding her head, she took a few steps back until she was in the middle of the kitchen's main area. Omar looked at her, hoping she wasn't about to get to going apeshit, when she reached behind her neck and untied her dress strap. Her dress fell to her feet then. Omar's eyes went wide with lustful desires. She was completely bare underneath. Her breasts called to him. The pussy pleaded for him. Her lips smiled at him.

"Stop bullshitting and come get this good pussy, Omar."

Unable to resist a bad bitch with a bomb on the neck, a wet ass pussy, and a fat ass, Omar's feet carried him before he even realized he was moving.

"Drop 'em, Mister," she demanded.

He obeyed and dropped his shorts and his boxers. His dick fell right out as stiff as a diving board. Claudia smiled at it, wrapped her hand around it, and gave it a gentle squeeze. She slowly stroked it with firm pressure. Omar groaned, eyes closing, anticipation growing by the second.

The next thing he knew, Claudia was on her knees before him. He opened his eyes, dying to watch and feel her. She held his dick off to the side and put her lips to his nuts. She kissed them, then opening her mouth, she stuck her tongue out and licked all over them.

He caught goosebumps and cursed repeatedly when she sucked his balls into her mouth and pleasured them with it. "Shit! Holy fuck, yo!" Omar cursed.

Claudia giggled. She loved making him feel good. It made her pussy leak like a paper towel trying to hold water that was poured on it. She was a natural born pleaser and didn't hide it. She spit his balls out, then she engulfed him. Omar's head spun in circles, while she deep throated him.

He grabbed her head and started fucking her face. His balls slapped her chin over and over again. Claudia moaned as he thotted her out.

"*Fuck*! Ohh, shit!" he shouted the second he felt his nut beginning to rise.

He kept fucking her face until the last second, then letting her head go, Omar pulled his dick out of her mouth. She opened wide, stuck her tongue out, and let him cum all over her face by stroking his joint inches away from it. The hot droplets splattered on her mug. She loved it. It made her feel like such a dirty, little whore that had the most handsome, Black man ever wrapped around her finger. Where there was pussy, there was power, and Claudia knew it.

She stood up from the floor. The look on his face told her that Kayla didn't exist in his mind at the moment. She stepped over to the sink and quickly washed the sperm away. She went back to him, finding him still stuck.

"How about we take this to your bed and handle stress the way we've always done before yo' woman gets back?" Claudia suggested, taking his hand into hers.

Nodding, though on autopilot, Omar pulled his boxers and shorts back up, then Claudia yanked him along, making sure that nothing but her jiggling ass was in his line of sight, while she took him up to his room to get really nasty.

***

Kayla frowned when she saw the number on the screen of her iPhone. She was in a fitting room, trying on something sooo very provocative that she knew the second Omar saw her in it, he was likely to bust a nut in his boxer briefs. The phone call interrupted her. She picked her phone up and reluctantly answered.

"You really got some screws loose, don't you? Why is you callin' me after you just left a bitch hangin'?"

154

"Maaan, I'm sorry, Kayla. I'ma keep it a 'hunnid wit'chu', joe. I's cleanin' that nigga's room out and lost myself," she heard Beast say.

"Aye, my man! Check it out! Where I'm from, money ain't more important than makin' sure ya squad is safe and together, yo! Homiez, you foul for that! You think cause you saved my life that I'ma let you get down on me like I'm a peon? Fuck outta here wit' that, nigga! I'm hangin' up!"

"Kayla! Hold up! Hear me out real quick! Please!"

She groaned, so close to breathing fire. She wanted to hang up, but the man had really saved her life. She felt indebted to him, and it irked her.

"What, Beast?"

"Look. Help me move some of this merch, and I'll cut you in. I swear on my mama I will, joe."

"Beast, yo, I am sooo very far from needin' money. I am all the way good."

"Aight. Then don't do it for the money. Do it cause a nigga see you and know he can trust you. Do it cause a nigga appreciates a real ass chick in his surroundings; more than all the fake creep ass niggas that think they some real street niggas. Kayla, I need yo' help. Can you please help me wit' this? Please?"

Kayla sighed to herself. She shook her head, hating that the nigga just had to have been the one to save her instead of Omar.

"Aight, yo. I'll help, but I need a few hours. I'm out wit' my girls, then I gotta go back to my man."

"Yo' man?" he questioned.

"Yeah, nigga. M-A-N. Mine. I'll hit you when I'm free."

She ended the call before he questioned her any further then set her phone down. Looking back in the mirror at herself, she smiled at the irresistibly gorgeous woman she saw.

"Wait 'til my nigga see me in this! Mhmm! We gon' get it on 'n poppin' over and over again!" she told herself then just thinking of another hot and crazy round had her getting hot like someone turned the heat up in the little fitting room.

***

Nate had just finished up whipping the last quarter kilo of crack, while Dirty chopped up tens, twenties, thirties, forties, and fifties for Eddie to bag up. In the dining room adjoined to the crack kitchen, Nate's brother, Max, and his crew were mixing up dope with cinnamon and fentanyl. Max broke down the five bricks that Nate got hit with on consignment from his connect out in New Jersey. Fresh in, Nate and Max were eager to get the shit out on the streets to get their money back. The two had built a long list of clients that wanted weight but still had plenty of snaps on the streets. The Lincoln-Larimer neighborhood had been real good to them, and they had no plans on letting anyone else step into their hood and get a dime of what was theirs and only theirs.

In a house in Larimer, close to the corner of Dean Street and Paulson Avenue, Nate and his brother's homies put their demos together and had everything bagged and ready to get pumped. They were ready to roll over to the basketball courts on Larimer, across the bridge, heading toward East Liberty. The doorbell rang as they all strapped up and tucked Glocks and Desert Eagles in their waistlines.

"Fuck is that?" Nate wondered to himself.

"Aye, Heavy, go get the door, yo," Max told his mans. "And if it's my baby mama, do not let her know I'm here, cutty. Real rap."

Heavy, a man as wide and tall as an oak wood door, went to do as his homie told him. Through the glass pane blocks in the double doors, Heavy saw a chick with bright blonde hair. He unlocked all four security locks and the chain lock. Standing there was a pretty ass chick with deep brown skin, like Hershey's chocolate, blonde hair in a ponytail, wearing a woman's, Ralph Lauren, polo shirt, tight denim jeans, and

Air Forces on her feet. Heavy felt like he was looking at the first lady of Ruff Ryderz back when she played the temperamental character, Terri, on the movie, *Barbershop*.

She had two bags in her hands, both with Giant Eagle – Pittsburgh's main and biggest supermarket grocery chain on them.

"Door Dash. I have ya order, sir," she said with some sassy attitude.

"Ain't nobody order that shit, yo. Wrong address,' Heavy told her.

"Hmm… are you sure?" she asked him with a raised eyebrow.

"Yeah. Yup."

Suddenly, a big man in jeans, Tims, a hoodie, and no mask on stepped into view, gripping a semi-automatic twelve-gauge shotgun with a drum.

"How bout this?!" he said and pulled the trigger.

***

Boom! Boom! Boom!

Tuck blew giant holes in the man, painting the doorway crimson. The blasts were loud as hell. The clock had started. Nala grabbed two Uzis from the bags she had, both with fifty-round clips, and got ready to run it.

Boc! Boc! Boc! Boc! Boc! Boc!

Shots came flying at her from inside the house.

Bocka! Bocka! Bocka! Bocka!

Bullets flew out of the living room's big window. Tuck grabbed Nala and kept her close to him, using the brick exterior wall between the front door and the window as cover. The shooting continued. They both remained calm, knowing mistakes were made when people moved too fast.

"Y'all niggaz got me fucked up, yo!" they heard one of them shout. "Run y'all asses up in here! Come on!"

"He sounds mad," Nala whispered to Tuck.

"Definitely does. Wanna make him see red?"
Nala laughed. "Yup."

***

"Harlem! Check outside the window! Dirty! Eddie! Y'all niggaz hit the front door! Start dumpin' on ya way out and Harlem gon' use the distraction y'all make to get they ass!" Nate demanded, coming up with a quick plan to get them and their merch out of the house before the cops get there; a big police station was less than ten minutes away.

While Nate and his brother held duffel bags full of dope and crack, the three hopped to it. Harlem crept to the shot-out window, gripping his Desert Eagle, and crouched down next to it, hidden from the outside. Dirty and Eddie hurried down the hall to the front door. They counted to three then together let their Glocks bark, as they ran out of the house to the porch where Heavy laid in a pool of blood.

Harlem jumped the second he heard the shots. He hurried to find a target but only saw Dirty and Eddie. Both were looking around for the shooters, but nobody was there.

"They ran, yo!" Dirty shouted, turning back toward the house as did Eddie.

Harlem looked back at Nate and Max, who were ready to haul ass up out of there. He shrugged at them then turned back toward Dirty and Eddie just as he discovered where the shooters had gone.

"Oh, shit! Aye, yo, watch…"
Brrrrrrrrr!
Brrrrrrrrr!

***

Tuck held onto Nala's ankles, as she flipped down from the roof over the porch with her Uzis. They had used the iron bars in the front of the porch's brick pillars to climb up to the second-floor windows right before more gunshots sounded off. Nala popped both of the shooters on the porch with her twin machine guns then caught the man in the window, as he attempted to dump on her.

She shook her legs and hollered for Tuck to let go. Reluctantly, he did. Nala acrobatically flipped down from the overhang and landed on her feet. Without wasting a second, as sirens started wailing from not too far away, she ran up the steps, into the house, guns up, trained to lock onto whoever remained alive.

"Bitch!" she heard a guy shout.

Nala whipped her head to the right and saw a big dreadhead on the steps to the second-floor, pointing a Desert Eagle at her. She dove for the floor, as he let off a shot that came so close to knocking a big plug out her ass that she felt the heat it had.

Boom! Boom! Boom! Boom!

She heard Tuck's semi-auto shotty blast four times. She looked up in time to see the dreadhead tumbling down the stairs with one arm and half a head. Tuck ran down the stairs with four duffel bags and his gauge.

"Come on! Let's go!" he shouted and bolted for the door.

Nala ran and caught up with Tuck, as he reached the door.

Bocka! Bocka! Bocka! Bocka! Bocka!

***

"Fuuuuck!" Nate yelled angrily when he missed taking the chick's head off before she made it out of the door.

He ran down the stairs, passing his blown apart brother. Running out of the house, he saw the two run toward a small car parked a couple of houses up. He fired at them again and again and again but still missed. Not willing to give up, Nate ran off the porch and down the sidewalk into the middle of the street right as the car's wheels smoked, as the driver mashed the gas.

Bocka! Bocka! Bocka! Bocka! Bocka! Bocka!

He blew the rear window out, but the car didn't stop. It flew down Paulson, hitting the hill, and disappeared from his sight.

Skkrrrrrr!

Nate jumped when he heard tires skidding behind him. He turned around with his gun and saw an unmarked police car there, doors flying open, two female cops hopping out.

"Drop the gun! Drop it! *Now!*" one yelled, pointing her gun at him.

"Don't shoot! I'm droppin' it, yo!" he shouted, then Nate dropped his gun and put his hands up.

***

Boc! Boc! Boc! Boc! Boc!

Mercilessly, Amber lit the man up like a Christmas tree. He fell backwards, dead before he even hit the ground.

"Rest in peace, bitch!" Amber shouted, then as fast as they had come, without sirens or strobes when they heard the shots fired call at one of the addresses Amber had given to Tuck to kick the door in, they dipped off, bee-lining down Dean Street, disappearing from the scene before the other cops that were closing in showed up.

***

"Yeeeeaah! Haahaaa! That's what the fuck I'm talking about! *Wooo!"* Nala cheered, as Tuck raced across the bridge, shooting up Larimer Avenue toward East Liberty.

Tuck chuckled, loving her enthusiasm. He was geeked as well. The bags felt very heavy. Nala went to take her blonde ponytail wig off when he stopped her.

"Hey, hey, hold up a sec, baby. Keep that on for a few more minutes," he told her.

She looked at him, puzzled, but then understood, as he undid his jeans and pulled his dick out. All too willingly, Nala got up on her knees in the seat of the stolen Chevy Aveo, leaned over the center console, lowering her head with her mouth wide open, and took his hard cock into her mouth, happy to treat her nigga to some bomb-ass neck for a job well done.

Chapter 16

Excited as hell, Kayla stepped out of the high-end salon, looking like a whole new woman. She couldn't wait for Omar to see her. He was going to go bananas.

"Guuuurl, that nigga gon' get cha' ass pregnant today, yo! On the Homiez, Kay!" Chante exclaimed, excited for Kayla.

Jerrica and Valerie agreed. Neither of them had ever seen their homegirl get dolled up for any man, and they had all been down since day one. Frankly, they all bet that Omar wouldn't even recognize her. She looked like a model ready to hit the runway in Paris. Her outfit and her sexy stilettos were the icing on the cake that they all knew Omar was going to devour.

"I don't know about all that, buuut I don't think I would stop him from tryin'," Kayla replied, as they all headed toward where the Hellcat Durango and Jerrica's Bentley truck were parked.

"You really think you could?" Valerie asked.

"Nope!" Jerrica answered for her, hitting the button on her key fob to start her Bentayga's engine.

"Shut up, Jerri. I believe she was asking me, wench."

"Aye, I don't know how long we gon' be out this way, but how bout we have some fun? Let's find a club to go to or at least a decent bar," Chante suggested.

"Y'all can do whatever y'all want. I will be chillin' wit' my dude at the crib wit' Smoke and Haze," Kayla replied right as they reached the SUVs. "Aye, Jerri. Bet'chu I'll smoke that Bentley truck in this joint."

Kayla remote started the Durango and got goosebumps from the sound.

"Bet!" Jerrica accepted the challenge and jumped into her Bentayga with Valerie, while Kayla jumped into the Hellcat truck with Chante.

They both peeled out of the lot, leaving behind rubber and smoke, racing through the streets of Gurnee like speeding was legal. They got back to Omar's house in mere minutes. Turning into the driveway, Kayla rolled toward the house and saw Smoke and Haze with two other dogs first, laid out on the front lawn, enjoying the sunlight. Her eyebrows furrowed at the two other dogs, then she saw a new, red Cadillac Escalade parked in front of Omar's porch.

"Who whip is that?" Chante asked, as Kayla parked behind it.

"Probably one of his friends. They gon' have to pack it up cause I needs me some alone time wit' him."

Kayla killed the engine, and they got out right as all four dogs ran up.

"Cheater!" Jerrica shouted when she and Valerie got out of the Bentayga.

"Ya mama, biatch!" Kayla patted Smoke and Haze's heads, then seeing the other two dogs, both females, were giddy with excitement as well, she patted them next.

Then, it hit her.

"Hold up… These gotta be Claudia's dogs."

"Who?" Chante asked.

Suddenly, Kayla took off running toward the front door, moving like she had on running shoes and not five-inch heels.

"Kay!" she heard Jerrica yell after her.

With her mind full of images that she prayed would not be real, Kayla burst into the house and immediately heard music playing loudly. She could make out the words to Saweetie's *NANI.* It was coming from the bedrooms.

Her girls and the dogs caught up to her, but not even a second later, she took off again, racing toward the music, fists already balled up and ready to swing.

***

"Mmmmm," Omar moaned under Claudia, sucking her pussy, while she sat on his face, leaned down, sucking his dick.

She leaked like a broken faucet into his mouth, while his dick pulsated in hers. Going crazy on each other in the sixty-nine position, Omar became engrossed in a fierce competition with Claudia, trying to make her cum before she made him cum.

Spending the last two hours going at it, the two had gotten lost in each other. Their high sex drives matched each other's. Their need to satisfy the other was unstoppable. Omar tried to fall back after the first nut, but when Claudia went face down, ass up, who the hell could say no to all that wet ass pussy and all that ass? The flesh was soooo motherfucking weak!

Omar slurped and sucked Claudia's clit like it was made of candy. She tasted so good, even after she had climaxed five times, and she still was charged up for him.

Claudia's back arched up from the amazing oral skills he had. She held him at the base of his dick, and trying to make him nut first, she engulfed all of him, going balls deep. With him down her throat and her lips close to his nuts, Claudia started humming.

She felt Omar snort in her pussy and jump at the same time from the sudden, unexpected vibration that tickled the shit out of his balls. Then, she started going crazy – sucking wildly, deep throating, moaning – which continuously sent tingling sensations coursing through his scrotum.

Claudia felt him trying to moan, but as he did, his lips vibrated her pussy lips, which made her head spin around and around in circles. Omar's nut was coming. She could taste it. Claudia was about to climax. She shook and trembled, juices flowing like a bottle of Moet knocked over without a cork in it.

It hit her. She exploded, climaxing all over his face. Then, it hit him, and he exploded in her mouth. While he slurped her clean, Claudia jerked and sucked him until he was all the way empty, and her mouth was full. She released his cock from her mouth and sat upright, only to come face to face with Kayla standing just five feet away from her, wearing a crazy sexy, all white, lace, nearly see through bodysuit with an oval-shaped opening over the top of her breasts, an open back, with a white bra and white G-string concealing her nipples and her goodie box. The white stilettos on her feet were shiny like latex. Her hair and makeup had her looking so breathtakingly gorgeous. Claudia gasped from not only how remarkably beautiful Kayla looked, but also from how irate she was looking – like she was ready to start shooting.

Omar felt Claudia's womanhood clench up over him, as he continued drinking her up. Then, he swore he felt her freeze up then gasp right as he heard GloRilla's *I Love Her* start playing.

He went to lift her off him, to see what was wrong, when he heard Claudia scream then *crack*!

She flew off him, and he saw Kayla on Claudia's ass, beating her like she stole something. Jerrica, Chante, and Valerie had been at the door. One of them slammed it shut. He heard the dogs barking from the other side, likely Hennessy and Tesla, after hearing Claudia screaming for him.

"*Kayla!*" he shouted when he was able to find his voice, then finding the strength to move, Omar jumped up off the bed in an attempt to get Kayla off of Claudia.

She swung furiously on Claudia, beating her face up like it was a speed bag. Claudia cried for help, trying to block her face from Kayla's little but hard jaw breakers.

"Kayla, yo, chill!" Omar again shouted, as he reached the frenzied girlrilla.

He went to grab Kayla. She peeped him coming and jumped back. Surprised by her speed, Omar stood there, motionless, staring at her with shock etched on his face. Hennessy and Telsa barked continuously from outside of the room. On the floor, bleeding, lumped up, wailing loudly, Claudia had curled up into a naked ball.

"Kay, what the hell, Ma?" Omar asked her.

She craned her neck, looking at him like he was the craziest man on Earth.

"Excuse me?! You askin' me what the hell?" Kayla started walking toward him with bloody, balled up fists.

"Yo, yo, yo, Kayla, come on! Chill out, ba…"

"Omar! I swear to God, nigga, if you even think about calling me baby!"

She kept walking toward him. He started backpedaling toward the wall, trying to avoid her.

"I'm sorry! Homiez, Kayla! I just…"

"Just what? Huh? You slipped and fell then she fell on ya face?"

His back was against the wall a second later. He tried to dart to the left, but Kayla was fast.

Wham!

She swung a hard right hook and rocked Omar's jaw. His head went to his right. She caught him with a left and sent his head back to his left. Omar fell on his ass and put his hands over his face to block her, as she swung wildly on him, trying to flood his ass.

"You fuckin' dickhead bastaaarrrd!" she screamed, going completely insane on him.

Crack!

A hard object bashed her in the back of the head, hard enough to send her flying forward to the floor, face first. Dazed but still lucid, Kayla rolled over onto her back just in time to see Claudia rush at her with a wooden cigar box in her hand, screaming like a homicidal maniac.

"Claudia, nooo!" Omar shouted, still on the floor. Kayla shot her right foot up and kicked Claudia in her gut when she got close enough. Claudia screamed from the blow. Dropping the box, she doubled over in pain. Kayla spun herself and kicked Claudia's legs from under her. She flipped backwards and hit the floor.

Bam!

The door flew opened and smacked the wall hard. Hennessy and Telsa ran in, quickly assessing the situation, seeing their human on the floor, battered and bleeding. Their eyes locked onto Kayla, and they charged.

"Hennessy! Tesla! Heel!" Omar commanded them, but they ignored him. Their owner's safety was in danger.

Jerrica, Chante, and Valerie ran in, pistols in their hands, pointing at the two female beasts.

"Smoke! Haze! Get 'em!" Omar shouted to his dogs, running toward Kayla to shield her from Claudia's dogs.

Before she could get up and run, Omar dove on top of her, using his body to protect her from the powerful killers. She then heard what sounded like fists hitting a chest, instantaneously followed by the eardrum piercing cries of more than one dog and the vicious growling. Claudia screamed, as Smoke and Haze grabbed her dogs by their necks and chomped down hard, yanking them back, away from Omar and Kayla.

"Omar! Stop them! Stop theem!" cried Claudia, watching his dogs get in position to kill hers.

"Release!" he shouted to them.

Obediently, Smoke and Haze let go of Hennessy and Tesla. The two females immediately laid down, blood pouring from the bite wounds in their necks. Smoke and Haze stood over them, growling viciously, as if they were daring them to move an inch.

Kayla caught Omar off-guard with a headbutt to his jaw. His bell rang. His head snapped back, and she managed to push him up off of her.

"Kayla, hold on, baby, please!" Omar begged.

"I told you not to call me that! I'm not ya fucking baby!" she hissed, getting up on her feet. "I'm not ya fuckin' girl, and I am not ya fuckin' friend! You are dead to me, Omar! *Dead*!"

She stomped toward the door, as her homegirls stepped to the side, but then, she stopped and turned around. Seeing Omar there, stuck in disbelief, broke her heart. Her eyes filled with tears. The pain in her heart was worse than the bullets that hit her leg and thigh. He stared back at her. Tears rolled down his face. He wanted to say something, but what could he?

Hearing movement, Kayla saw Claudia trying to stand. She saw red. Heated to the point that she was nearly about to breathe fire, Kayla charged Claudia and bum-rushed her like she was a linebacker. She rushed Claudia all the way to the glass French doors that opened to his bedroom's lounging patio deck. She pushed with all of her might and sent her sailing, crashing through the glass, landing on her back on huge shards of it. Her screams were so loud. Shards of glass impaled her. Blood leaked and spewed from so many cuts. Claudia couldn't move. The pain was unbearable.

Kayla's nostrils flared with anger. She stared daggers into Claudia with violently painful death wishes rolling through her mind. She turned away, looking once more at Omar. He remained on the floor, staring up at her, dumbfounded.

"K-Kayla," he stammered.

She ignored him and headed toward the door. Hennessy and Tesla started growling. Smoke and Haze growled at them and shut them right up.

Ignoring Omar, she told her girls that they were out. Smoke and Haze tried to follow, whimpering sadly, sensing Kayla's furious departure. She turned to them. They begged with their eyes and whines for her to stay. Kayla leaned down and cupped each of them by their cheeks. She kissed their foreheads and told them she loved them, then she turned away and headed to leave out.

Devasted, Omar watched Kayla march out of his bedroom. He received enraged, dirty looks from Jerrica, Chante, and Valerie before they left out, running to catch up with Kayla.

"Fuck!" he cursed, mentally kicking his own ass for screwing up so badly.

Omar looked at his dogs. They sat, side by side, looking at him. Smoke growled at him. Haze grunted. Omar looked at the females. They were still laying on their stomachs, yielding to his dogs. Claudia cried for Omar to help her. The more she moved, the more the glass cut her.

"Hold on. Stop movin', Claudia," he told her.

Scraping himself up off of the floor, Omar stood with rubbery legs and went to help Claudia up. The second he stepped out to the patio, he heard the sounds of a twin-turbo, 12-cylinder engine revving then tires screeching as what he knew was Jerrica's Bentley truck peeled off with the only girl he had truly given his heart to racing away from him, breaking his heart and breaking him.

Chapter 17

"Daayum! This shit crazy, joe! On God, I just checked into cash!" Jerrod looked at the stack of money in his hand that he had acquired in just two hours.

He counted $1,850, all from his dope.

"Maaaan, fuck Kenosha! Westside best side!"

"Don't forget it neither, fam," said Lil E, one of the CVLs that Ice had called in to help Jerrod pump his dope.

Along with Lil E was Chiron, Money, and Ari. The four were accompanied by five chicks, all out there kicking it with money getters on the corner of 16th and Lawndale, posted in front of a restaurant.

Lil E had his chick, Reekah, with him. Chiron was with one of his breezies that people called Peanut due to her size and skin tone. Money was joined by Kiera, and Ari had Candance. The fifth chick's name was Amalia. She was Puerto Rican and Black, while the others were straight Black with different skin tones. Amalia was a beautiful petite red bone with burgundy-dyed hair, sporting a tight denim H&M miniskirt, white Air Jordan 6s on her feet, and a white belly top that let her flat stomach and pierced belly button show.

Amalia had been flirting with Jerrod since he got dropped off on the corner by Ice with Lil E, Money, and Ari. He was definitely digging her and couldn't wait until he sold off all of what he brought from Ice's crib. He had plans to trick a little bit of cash off, get a bottle, some good weed, blunts, a hotel, then take her there and smash.

"Westside is always gon' be the best side to get money on," Lil E added. "Be about the hustle and the money's gon' come, ya dig I'm sayin'?"

"I definitely do, my nigga," Jerrod nodded, flicking through his cash again. "Damn, this corner is pumpin'. It's like a busy car wash or somethin'."

Dope fiends walked up and pulled up every few minutes. Ever since Jerrod and the other guys got there, taking over for the group that was emptied out, one fiend bought a $10 bag of Jerrod's mix, and the next thing he knew, three more, including the first, came. Then seven came and then fifteen, on foot and in cars. Lil E and the others had pockets full of bags and quickly sold off what was quickly going around the area as the *fire ass* dope within thirty minutes. Jerrod had brought an ounce worth initially until Ice told him to bring more. So, he brought a quarter of a brick, half of it broken down into bags, the other half into chunks, more so for other dope boys that were definitely going to get some to cop and sell in other spots, which would bring Jerrod even more business via word of mouth.

"Thank yo' uncle for this, fam," Chiron told him, walking up with a couple hundred more in his hand for Jerrod. "Everybody out hea' know he the king dopeman, even though he don't sell blow. If he puts his name on it or swea's upon it, then it's law. You gon' sell the whole two bricks by tonight or tomorrow damn near, joe."

"On the Five," Money agreed then headed toward where a fiend had just pulled up with more money.

"Damn, baby, you just got out hea', and you doin' real good," came Amalia, strutting toward Jerrod like a model with Jordans on her feet.

"I'm that nigga, shorty. Yain' know?" Jerrod grinned at her, still flicking through his bankroll, which now was at just over two grand in two hours and ten minutes.

"I see. You turnin' into an overnight celebrity out this muhfucka, joe. We gon' kick it tonight still?"

Closing the gap between them, Amalia's breasts touched Jerrod's sternum. Her sweet perfume wafted into his nostrils, and her perky lips had him lusting hard. Even though she was petite, she still had a nice little ass that was round and had Jerrod dying to hit it from the back, while he pulled her hair and smacked all over it.

"Oh, yeah. We gotta find som fi' to smoke on too, but I really wanna sell off as much of my shit as I can before I get to kickin' back," he told her just as his phone started ringing.

Jerrod asked her to hold up a second when he saw who it was. He answered right away.

"Whaz hanin'?"

"Where are you?" he heard Kayla ask.

She sounded pissed!

"Uh… Chicago… out west. You aight?"

"No! Go in ya locator app and send me where you are! I'm on the way to you, yo!"

Jerrod couldn't ignore the fury in her voice. Apprehensive about her sudden demand to know where he was and her eagerness to get to him made him think the jig was up. That she knew that he was EBK and that everything that had happened since the night she was at the Culver's was all because of him.

"Talk to me, Kayla. You obviously upset. Did I do something? Keep it a buck wit' me, shorty."

"Nigga, if I was hot wit' you, I wouldn't be callin' to find out where you are! I'd pull up and dump on you! It's real easy to find someone these days, Beast, so either we linkin' up to get on that business or I'm goin' the fuck back to my city! You got five seconds to decide, nigga!"

"Aight, damn, Kayla, relax!" Jerrod went into the app she spoke of and sent her his location. "You get it?" he asked afterwards.

"Yeah."

The call ended without another word.

"That's yo' woman?"

Jerrod put his phone in his pocket and looked at Amalia. She had a hand on her hip, lips twisted, and eyebrow raised. "Naw, shorty. My heart ain't for sale. My dick is though." She started smiling at that.

"Must be good if you think it's worth money. How bout you give me a free sample, then I'll either be back for more or I'll be goin' elsewhere?"

Jerrod laughed. "I got that dope dick, lil mama. Ain't no goin' to someone else for better, but lemme get a little bit more of this merch sold, then we can hit it."

"Or you can pack up now, I take you to get what you got left, and my people will buy all of it right on the spot. And they got supa' fi'ass exotic we can roll up and blaze, baby. What chu' say?"

She licked her glossy lips suggestively, and at the same time, she reached and grabbed Jerrod's crotch, squeezing his dick, feeling how ready he was to get with the program.

"Okay. Yeah. We can do that. I ain't got a whip though, so…"

"I got my car here, Jerrod. Quit stallin'."

She pulled out the keys to her 2008 Pontiac G8 GXP and pointed toward where her red four-door was parked. "I don't have a license, so you gotta drive."

"Sheit, I ain't got Ls either, shorty, but I'm thuggin'." Jerrod grabbed the keys from her. "Go on ahead and get in. I'll be right thea', shorty."

***

After Jerrod collected what dope he had left and his money from Lil E and his Lord homies – much to their dismay since the shit was moving a mile a minute – he went and got behind the wheel of Amalia's Pontiac.

"Here. Hold this down for me, shorty." Jerrod handed her the mini duffel that had the dope in it then started the V8 engine that rested under the hood of the car.

"Oh, and take yo time too, boo-boo," Amalia said, stuffing the bag under her seat.

"Take my time? You sounded real eager a minute ago," he chuckled, putting it into drive and pulling away from the curb.

Amalia reached over and started undoing his jeans.

"Ohh... okay then!" Jerrod excitedly added.

She took his gun and put it on the floorboard in front of her seat, and she got up on her knees. She pulled Jerrod's stiff cock out and wasted no time lowering her head, mouth open wide, and engulfing all of his dick until her lips reached the base.

"Woooo! Okay! Damn! Take my time! You got it, lil mama! Suck this muhfucka good, and I'ma take real good care of you when we get to the telly," Jerrod told her, then cruising at the speed limit, he reached around her to pull her skirt up and rub on her ass, while she domed him up. He made his way to Ice's spot to get the rest of his dope before going to meet with Amalia's people.

***

"Aye, we closed, ma'am," Doug told the chick at the door to his medium-sized soul food restaurant that sat on the corner of Frankstown Avenue and Homewood Avenue in Homewood.

She had been banging on the windows to the seating area, while his last two waitresses were cleaning up to shut down for the night. One of them had gone to get the boss, knowing that the night life around the area teemed with snaps, prostitutes, dope boys, and stick-up kids. A restaurant that did pretty well was a target in such a dilapidated hood, but the owner of the restaurant was far from a regular guy. He was very well connected.

Upon arriving at the front door, Doug saw the chocolate-brown skinned chick with long, green hair hanging loosely, a tight green, long-sleeved dress with ruffled sleeves, a ruffled cleavage line, and a flared thigh-length hem. She wore gold jewelry, gold eyeshadow, gold lipstick, a gold Versace watch, and had gold stilettos on her feet that accentuated her toned legs.

Doug found her to be a very beautiful woman, but most street walkers were. So, he brought along his Smith & Wesson semi-automatic .45 in case she happened to be a female on a mission to rob him of his wealth, ill-gotten or legit.

"I know. I know. I'm sorry, but my car broke down up the street, and I gotta use the bathroom soooo damn bad! Pleeaase, can I use yours?" she begged, nearly on the brink of tears.

She danced around in the spot she stood in, visibly in distress.

"Okay. Come on inside. You can use my bathroom, but then you gotta go."

"Okay! Can we go? I'm bout to explode!"

Doug stepped aside and let her in. He called his waitresses over and instructed them to take the girl to the bathroom then show her out. They nodded their heads and did as told. Doug watched them lead the girl away, hearing her groaning and cursing with discomfort, her heels tapping loudly on the tile floor.

He headed back to his office to finish counting his money. Closing and locking the door, Doug sat back at his desk. He glanced at the security camera monitor screen and saw the various spots his cameras surveilled. He saw Fantasia and Normandie posted outside of the bathroom, waiting for the girl.

Turning his head, he got back to the piles of cash on his desk, the result of making ten kilos of cocaine disappear throughout the week, and he still had fifteen left in his safe with buyers already in line for them. Turning his music back up, Doug fed another stack into the money counter. Ten

CHRISTOPHER "DIESEL" HORNEZES

grand more brought the number up to $123, 500 with one more stack to go. After he fed the last stack in then rubber banded it, Doug glanced at the security monitor and saw one of the waitresses emerge from the bathroom with a plastic bag in her hand, looking downwards, as she scurried away.

"Aw, come on, man! I know she didn't mess my muthafuckin' bathroom up, yo!"

Doug got up and made his way to the door. After he unlocked both locks, he opened it and stepped out.

Wham!

"Aaahhh, shit!" he screamed when a wooden bat came swinging and hit him in his ribs, cracking one instantly.

He dropped to the floor and saw a big, dark-brown skinned man standing over him, holding the bat in his hands.

"Aye, yo, my man?" he said, then without even waiting for a response, he raised the bat up high over his head.

"No! Wait!"

***

Tuck brought the bat down as hard as he could on Doug's left knee, obliterating it completely. Doug screamed in pain, grabbing for his busted knee, while still clutching his broken rib. Just then, Nala appeared, wearing one of the waitress' uniforms. She dragged the two unconscious waitresses behind her by their hands, using every ounce of muscle she had to do so. One was half-naked, left only in her bra and panties. Tuck smiled as she came to a stop. He only wished he could have seen her immobilize them. For such a small chick, Nala could do damage. She had hands that were fueled with high-octane and anger problems.

"Remind me to cook for you when this is over," he told her.

"Naw, yo, you can't cook for shit," she replied, putting her hands on her hips, "but if you really wanna show me

176

love, then do what SWV says and go doooowntooown, cause it's the way to my love."

Tuck laughed his ass off, ignoring Doug and his crying.

"You got that, baby. Let's get this money and go," he told her.

Grabbing Doug by his right foot, Tuck dragged him into the office. Nala dragged the waitresses in then closed the door behind them.

"Bingo!" Tuck saw all the money on the desk and lit up with excitement. "Now this a easy ass lick! Let's get it all and be out."

"Bae."

Tuck looked at Nala, mid-step. She was pointing at something. He turned and looked. He saw a tall, old school, steel safe with a combination lock in the corner.

"Oohh, wouldja look at that! Damn, I almost ain't see that joint."

Tuck looked down at Doug.

"Aye, bro. Check it out. The pain you experiencin' right now ain't shit compared to what you gon' feel if you lie about what's in the safe and if you act like you forgot the combination. Do you understand?"

Shaking from the crippling pain shooting throughout his body like a festering wound, Doug looked up at him through eyes filled with hatred and malice.

"You a dead man, Tuck! Homiez!" he hissed angrily. "My nigga, O, gon' murder ya wannabe ass, bitch nigga! On Crip, yo!"

"Oh, snap! The shit in the safe belongs to O? Aw, yeah! I needs all of it! What the combination, bruh?"

"O-One... two... fuck... you!"

Tuck homerun slammed Doug's right knee. He cried in pain at the top of his lungs.

Nala started getting antsy. She hated licks that weren't in and out, especially when they were on high rollers or high rollers that worked for bosses. Clutching her gun tightly in her hand, she considered telling Tuck to just get the money, but before she could, the alarm suddenly started going off, and lights began flashing.

"Shit! What the fuck happened?" Tuck demanded, looking around the office.

Nala peeked outside of the office. She didn't see anyone in the hallway.

"Just get the money! We need to go!" she urged him.

"Man, I need the safe opened up! I know there's dope in it."

Boc! Boc! Boc!

"Aaaahhhh, fuuuuuuuck!"

Nala gasped in shock when Doug managed to pull out a pistol from the small of his back and put three bullets into Tuck's ass. She instantly took aim at him before he could fire again and emptied her entire clip into his chest and his face.

Tuck screamed in pain. He hopped around, holding his rear end like it was on fire.

"Bae! Oh, my God!" she panicked, running to his side.

"Get th-the money! Get the money!" he yelled, pigeon-toe waddling toward the wall.

"But Tu…"

"Money!" he roared, cutting her off.

She hurried to do as demanded. Rushing as fast as she could, Nala found a big red Gucci duffel bag and stuffed every dollar in it. She went to Tuck, took his arm, and let him loop it over her shoulder, then helped him toward the restaurant's front, praying to God that they made it out before the cops showed up.

***

Sitting in their black unmarked Impala, Amber and Cammie watched from the parking lot of a closed-down KFC across from *Doug's Soul Food Kitchen.* They heard the security alarm blaring and saw the lights inside flashing.

People around the area paid little to no attention to the restaurant, too busy trying to score dope, coke, weed, or just out there kicking it.

Seconds later, they saw who they knew was Tuck and his little ride or die bitch smash out the glass in the front door and exit. Tuck hobbled out, and the girl, who had a duffel bag strap on her shoulder, assisted him.

"Looks like someone finally got his ass," said Amber with a slight chuckle.

"Literally!" laughed Cammie.

After the two disappeared into the shadows of the line of tall bushes on the restaurant's property line, Amber heard the call for burglary alarm check come over the radio. Starting the engine, she put it in drive and pulled off, exiting the parking lot and dipping off, leaving the area before any other squads could show up.

Chapter 18

Jerrod was happy to see that Ice wasn't home, nor were his ladies. He hopped out of Amalia's car after parallel parking. Hurrying into his uncle's crib using the keys Ice gave him, Jerrod went and got the rest of the dope he had, and he grabbed the diamond jewelry that he had taken from Knuck, planning to somehow pop it all off whenever Kayla arrived.

Running back out, Jerrod locked the house up then got back behind the wheel. Amalia told him which way to go. Following her directions, Jerrod made his way north up Avers to 18th then hopped onto the one-way to take it west. When he came to Karlov, Amalia told him they were less than a minute away.

Arriving at the entrance to the lot of some projects, Jerrod saw so many people outside like a block party was being held. He saw nearly everyone that had a hat on had it either banged to the right or they were blue.

"Where are we?" he asked Amalia, noticing how everybody was looking their way, as if the car had a flag with Donald Trump's face on it hanging on its sides.

"I live here. My uncle and his people call it The Square. Park by that blue Escalade over there," she pointed out.

Jerrod saw the SUV sitting on big rims. He rolled toward it and pulled into the parking spot next to it and a box Chevy on even bigger rims. The second he put it in park and went to cut the engine off, Jerrod heard screeching tires. Glancing in the rearview mirror, he saw a H2 Hummer SUT blocking him in.

"What the hell?"

Then, the doors flew open and out hopped a mob of guys. Jerrod instantly recognized the man that had gotten out of the front passenger's side – the chunky dude with the shit-lock dreads and bald spot that had been with Rob G when his uncle had taken him to meet Chino and his guys. Jerrod saw the man had a shotgun in his hands, as he rounded the back of the Pontiac.

"Oh, shit! Aye! Gimme my g…"

Click clack!

Jerrod's panicked request was halted when he heard the gun cock right next to his right ear.

"Unlock the door," he heard Amalia demand, pressing the barrel of his own gun to his temple right as DY approached.

"Damn, shorty, that's what chu' on? You gon' suck a nigga dick, swallow his kids, then set me up?"

"It worked, didn't it?"

"You's a cold bitch, joe. On God, yo' ass cold."

"Uh huh. Cry me a river, nigga, but while you do, open the door, so my baby daddy can have a word wit' you."

Jerrod unlocked the door. DY opened it and told him to get out. Glaring at the fat motherfucker, Jerrod did as told, encouraged by the business end of the 12-gauge.

"Hands up, nigga," DY told him.

Jerrod did as told. He was patted down by another man. Finding no gun or any other type of weapon, the guy nodded to DY.

"Aye, Rob!" DY hollered out.

Aw, come on, man! These Chicago niggas is grimy as fuck! Jerrod thought when he looked to his left, peeping that it was indeed Rob G's blue Hummer on the big twenty-sixes.

Rob G rounded the front end of the H2 a second later and walked right up to Jerrod. Amalia had gotten out and was handing the dope and the cash off to one of Rob's guys.

"Whaz hanin', fam? You aight? You look a little scared right now, joe," the O.G. said to Jerrod.

"Naw, bruh. I don't get scared. I'm a muhfuckin' gangsta," Jerrod replied, standing tall and fearless despite the rising number of Ganster Disciples surrounding him, all of them under Rob G's command.

"Oh, yeah? I heard you one of them EBK niggas," Rob G then said.

"EBK?" Jerrod's heart dropped to his feet at the mention of his real affiliation. "N-Naw, fam. I would never be in a mob like that. I get money. That it – that's all."

Rob G nodded his head. He dug in his pocket and pulled out his iPhone. Jerrod stood nervously, hearing him making a video call. DY was staring dead at him, holding the shotgun to his chest. The others that had hopped out of Rob G's whip were posted with semi-autos in their hands and mobbed up all around the lot, so many more thumped up, and all readily willing to do as the O.G. said.

"Aye, fam. Check it out," Rob G spoke when the call was answered.

He turned the screen toward Jerrod then. The second Jerrod saw who was on the screen, his eyes went wide in sheer shock. His face was badly burned, and by the collar of the gown he had on, Jerrod could tell he was in the hospital. There was no doubt in his mind he was looking at EBK Knuck – alive, breathing, not dead!

"This the nigga that stained you and went against the grain, folks?" Rob G asked him.

"Yeah, that's him, G. That's that snake-ass nigga. What up, Jerrod? Bet'chu thought you got rid of me, huh?"

Even with all the burns on his face, Knuck still managed to smirk at the dumbfounded Jerrod.

"Ain't got shit to say, bitch ass nigga? It's cool. You ain't gotta say shit. My people gon' talk for me, joe. Say yo' prayers, pussy."

"Don't 'een trip, nephew," Rob G then said, turning the phone's screen back toward him. "I'ma have this nigga beggin' for death, joe. He gon' see how the Brick Boyz get down. Mock, Rello, and Chuck on they way to come get him."

"Say less, Unc. Make sure you tell me where you bury his snake ass, so I can come piss on him."

"I got'chu, lil nigga."

Rob hit end and terminated the video call. He looked at Jerrod and smiled evilly at him. Jerrod swallowed hard. It was not looking good for him. His phone started ringing in his pocket. DY lowered the shotgun and went in Jerrod's pocket, pulling his phone out. He gave it to Rob and stood by.

"Who dis joe?" Rob answered, seeing the name Kayla on the screen, putting it on speaker.

"Who is this? Where's Beast at?" Jerrod heard her ask.

"Beast? This nigga ain' no muhfuckin' beast, shorty. In a minute, his ass gon' be worm food. You his bitch?"

The call ended. Jerrod saw Rob G's eyebrows furrow.

"Damn." Chuckling, Rob looked at Jerrod. "If that's yo' bitch, I feel sorry for you, joe. Now another nigga finna be dickin' her down, all cause you got cho'self murked," he said just as screeching tires filled the air.

"That's yo' ride up outta hea', fam. Nice knowin' you, joe. Don't 'een trip though. That nigga, Ice, Chino, and his guys gon' meet chu' thea."

Boc! Boc! Boc! Boc! Boc!

Boom! Boom! Boom! Boom!

Brrrrrrrr! Brrrrrrrr!

Brrrrrrrrrr! Brrrrrrrr!

Multiple gunshots suddenly rang out. Screaming and shouting from all around Jerrod filled the air. Rob G was immediately covered by five of his guys and rushed off toward the buildings, away from the shooting, like he was the president, and they were his secret service goons. The gunshots and the chaotic screaming and yelling was enough to distract DY. Jerrod seized the opportunity and ran up on the man.

Crack!

Jerrod caught him right in the jaw. The thunderous blow rocked him hard enough that he flew up against the Escalade. He rushed DY and swung repeatedly, bopping his fat ass up. DY, overwhelmed by the lightening fast swings, lost control of his grip on the shotgun and dropped it. Jerrod delivered one last hard blow to DY's kidney. DY yelped in pain as a loud, wet fart escaped him. When DY doubled over at the waist, Jerrod grabbed him by his little shit-locks, yanked his head down, and jumped at the same time, delivering a bone-crunching knee to the center of DY's face.

DY flew backwards, slamming into the Escalade, and then with a broken nose gushing blood, he dropped to the ground, face first, with a big brown stain at the seat of his Levi's jeans.

"Bitch ass nigga!" Jerrod spat, as the shooting continued.

Jerrod had no clue what the hell was going on. All he knew was that pandemonium had broken out all over the projects, and he had to get gone… fast.

Remembering the diamond jewelry was still in the car, he rushed to grab it from the side door pocket. Geeked that it was all still there, he hurried and grabbed the shotgun that DY no longer needed and pumped it, but as he went to dip off…

Wham!

He was hit hard in the back of the head. Yelping in pain from the blow, Jerrod flew forward and hit the ground. The shotgun flew out of his hand. He was dazed and sure he heard bells ringing.

"Aye, joe! Turn yo' bitch ass ova!"

Bleeding from the gaping wound in the back of his head, Jerrod muscled himself over onto his back. He looked up and saw Amalia there, pointing his cannon at his face.

"This is what happens when a snake ass, bitch ass nigga like you brings his dumbass into Kedvale Square!"

Bocka! Bocka! Bocka! Bocka! Bocka!

"Aaaaahhhhh!"

To Be Continued…

Lock Down Publications and Ca$h Presents
Assisted Publishing Packages

Due to an increase in the price of services we have increased our prices. The prices below reflect the price increase as of 11/1/24.

BASIC PACKAGE	UPGRADED PACKAGE
$699	$1000
Editing	Typing
Cover Design	Editing
Formatting	Cover Design
	Formatting
	Upload eBooks to Amazon
	Upload Paperback to Amazon
ADVANCE PACKAGE	**LDP SUPREME PACKAGE**
$1,400	$1,700
Typing	Typing
Editing (line editing/content)	Editing (line editing/content)
Cover Design	Cover Design
Formatting	Formatting
Copyright Registration	Copyright Registration
Proofreading	Proofreading
Upload eBooks to Amazon	Set up Amazon Account
Upload Paperback to Amazon	Upload eBooks to Amazon
	Upload Paperback to Amazon
	Advertise on LDP's Amazon and Facebook Page

***

Other services available upon request.
Additional charges may apply

Lock Down Publications
P.O. Box 944
Stockbridge, GA 30281-9998

Phone: 470 303-9761
Email: lockdownpublications@gmail.com

Submission Guideline

Submit the first three chapters of your completed manuscript to ldpsubmissions@gmail.com. In the subject line add **Your Book's Title**. The manuscript must be in a Word Doc file and sent as an attachment. Document should be in Times New Roman, double spaced, and in size 12 font. Also, provide your synopsis and full contact information. If sending multiple submissions, they must each be in a separate email.

Have a story but no way to send it electronically? You can still submit to LDP/Ca$h Presents. Send in the first three chapters, written or typed, of your completed manuscript to:

LDP: Submissions Dept
P.O. Box 944
Stockbridge, GA 30281-9998

DO NOT send original manuscript. Must be a duplicate. Provide your synopsis and a cover letter containing your full contact information.

Thanks for considering LDP and Ca$h Presents.

NEW RELEASES

BLOODLINE OF A SAVAGE 1-3
THESE VICIOUS STREETS 1-3
RELENTLESS GOON 1-3
BY PRINCE A. TAUHID

THE BUTTERFLY MAFIA 1-3
BY FUMIYA PAYNE

A THUG'S STREET PRINCESS 1&2
BY MEESHA

CITY OF SMOKE 3
BY MOLOTTI

GET IT IN SLUGS 1 &2
BY B. STALL

STANDING ON HER BUSINESS 1&2
BY DG SANTANA

STEPPERS 1,2&3
THE REAL BADDIES OF CHI-RAQ
BY KING RIO

THE LANE 1&2
BY KEN-KEN SPENCE

THUG OF SPADES 1&2
LOVE IN THE TRENCHES 2
CORNER BOYS
BY COREY ROBINSON

TIL DEATH 3
BY ARYANNA

CHRISTOPHER "DIESEL" HORNEZES

THE BIRTH OF A GANGSTER 4
BY DELMONT PLAYER

PRODUCT OF THE STREETS 1-3
BY DEMOND "MONEY" ANDERSON

NO TIME FOR ERROR
BY KEESE

MONEY HUNGRY DEMONS 1-2
BY TRANAY ADAMS

HUB CITY MENACE 1-3
BY J. WHITE

A THUGGISH PASSION 1&2
LAND OF DA HOOLIGANZ 1-4
KILLAZ ON STANDBY 1&2
BY IRA B.

FO'EVA ROLLIN 1&2
BY ASSA RAYMOND BAKER

THE LEVEL UP 1&3
BY LUXURY KING

Coming Soon from Lock Down Publications/Ca$h Presents

IF YOU CROSS ME ONCE 6
ANGEL V
By Anthony Fields

A THUGS STREET PRINCESS 3
By Meesha

CORNER BOYS 2
By Corey Robinson

THA TAKEOVER
By Keith Chandler

BETRAYAL OF A G 2
By Ray Vinci

SAVAGE FAMILY EMPIRE 1&2
SOULLESS GOON 1,2&3
THE DIRTY SIDE OF MONEY 1,2&3
By Prince

FOR MY ENEMY'S SAKE
AMBITIONS OF A SLIDER
FRESH OFF DA PORCH
By IRA B.

BY THE TRUCKLOAD 1-4
TIPPIN' THE SCALES 1-3
BAD BITCHES WIT GUNZ 3
PROBLEM SOLVED 2
By Christopher "Diesel" Hornezes

Available Now

RESTRAINING ORDER 1 & 2
By **CA$H & Coffee**

LOVE KNOWS NO BOUNDARIES 1-3
By **Coffee**

RAISED AS A GOON I, II, III & IV
BRED BY THE SLUMS I, II, III
BLAST FOR ME I & II
ROTTEN TO THE CORE I II III
A BRONX TALE I, II, III
DUFFLE BAG CARTEL I II III IV V VI
HEARTLESS GOON I II III IV V
A SAVAGE DOPEBOY I II
DRUG LORDS I II III
CUTTHROAT MAFIA I II
KING OF THE TRENCHES
By **Ghost**

LAY IT DOWN I & II
LAST OF A DYING BREED I II
BLOOD STAINS OF A SHOTTA I & II III
By **Jamaica**

LOYAL TO THE GAME I II III
LIFE OF SIN I, II III
By **TJ & Jelissa**

IF LOVING HIM IS WRONG…I & II
LOVE ME EVEN WHEN IT HURTS I II III
By **Jelissa**

PUSH IT TO THE LIMIT
By **Bre' Hayes**

THE GIRLRILLA AND HER N*GGA KAY-O

BLOODY COMMAS I & II
SKI MASK CARTEL I, II & III
KING OF NEW YORK I II, III IV V
RISE TO POWER I II III
COKE KINGS I II III IV V
BORN HEARTLESS I II III IV
KING OF THE TRAP I II
By **T.J. Edwards**

WHEN THE STREETS CLAP BACK I & II III
THE HEART OF A SAVAGE I II III IV
MONEY MAFIA I II
LOYAL TO THE SOIL I II III
By **Jibril Williams**

A DISTINGUISHED THUG STOLE MY HEART I II & III
LOVE SHOULDN'T HURT I II III IV
RENEGADE BOYS 1-4
PAID IN KARMA 1-3
SAVAGE STORMS 1-3
AN UNFORESEEN LOVE 1-3
BABY, I'M WINTERTIME COLD 1-3
A THUG'S STREET PRINCESS 1&2
By **Meesha**

A GANGSTER'S CODE 1-3
A GANGSTER'S SYN 1-3
THE SAVAGE LIFE 1-3
CHAINED TO THE STREETS 1-3
BLOOD ON THE MONEY 1-3
A GANGSTA'S PAIN 1-3
BEAUTIFUL LIES AND UGLY TRUTHS
CHURCH IN THESE STREETS
By **J-Blunt**

CUM FOR ME 1-8
An LDP Erotica Collaboration

BLOOD OF A BOSS 1-5
SHADOWS OF THE GAME
TRAP BASTARD
By **Askari**

THE STREETS BLEED MURDER 1-3
THE HEART OF A GANGSTA 1-3
By **Jerry Jackson**

WHEN A GOOD GIRL GOES BAD
By **Adrienne**

THE COST OF LOYALTY 1-3
By **Kweli**

BRIDE OF A HUSTLA 1-3
THE FETTI GIRLS 1-3
CORRUPTED BY A GANGSTA 1-4
BLINDED BY HIS LOVE
THE PRICE YOU PAY FOR LOVE 1-3
DOPE GIRL MAGIC 1-3
By **Destiny Skai**

A KINGPIN'S AMBITION
A KINGPIN'S AMBITION II
I MURDER FOR THE DOUGH
By **Ambitious**

TRUE SAVAGE 1-7
DOPE BOY MAGIC 1-3
MIDNIGHT CARTEL 1-3
CITY OF KINGZ 1&2
NIGHTMARE ON SILENT AVE
THE PLUG OF LIL MEXICO 1&2
CLASSIC CITY
By **Chris Green**

THE GIRLRILLA AND HER N*GGA KAY-O

A GANGSTER'S REVENGE 1-4
THE BOSS MAN'S DAUGHTERS 1-5
A SAVAGE LOVE 1&2
BAE BELONGS TO ME 1&2
A HUSTLER'S DECEIT 1-3
WHAT BAD BITCHES DO 1-3
SOUL OF A MONSTER 1-3
KILL ZONE
A DOPE BOY'S QUEEN 1-3
TIL DEATH 1-3
IMMA DIE BOUT MINE 1-6
DYING FOR LIKES
By **Aryanna**

A DOPEBOY'S PRAYER
By **Eddie "Wolf" Lee**

THE KING CARTEL 1-3
By **Frank Gresham**

THESE NIGGAS AIN'T LOYAL 1-3
By **Nikki Tee**

GANGSTA SHYT 1-3
By **CATO**

THE ULTIMATE BETRAYAL
By **Phoenix**

BOSS'N UP 1-3
By **Royal Nicole**

I LOVE YOU TO DEATH
By **Destiny J**

I RIDE FOR MY HITTA
I STILL RIDE FOR MY HITTA
By **Misty Holt**

CHRISTOPHER "DIESEL" HORNEZES

LOVE & CHASIN' PAPER
By **Qay Crockett**

TO DIE IN VAIN
SINS OF A HUSTLA
By **ASAD**

BROOKLYN HUSTLAZ
By **Boogsy Morina**

BROOKLYN ON LOCK 1 & 2
By **Sonovia**

GANGSTA CITY
By **Teddy Duke**

A DRUG KING AND HIS DIAMOND 1-3
A DOPEMAN'S RICHES
HER MAN, MINE'S TOO 1&2
CASH MONEY HO'S
THE WIFEY I USED TO BE 1&2
PRETTY GIRLS DO NASTY THINGS
By **Nicole Goosby**

LIPSTICK KILLAH 1-3
CRIME OF PASSION 1-3
FRIEND OR FOE 1-3
By **Mimi**

TRAPHOUSE KING 1-3
KINGPIN KILLAZ 1-3
STREET KINGS 1&2
PAID IN BLOOD 1&2
CARTEL KILLAZ 1-3
DOPE GODS 1&2
By **Hood Rich**

THE STREETS ARE CALLING

THE GIRLRILLA AND HER N*GGA KAY-O

By **Duquie Wilson**

STEADY MOBBN' 1-3
THE STREETS STAINED MY SOUL 1-3
By **Marcellus Allen**

WHO SHOT YA 1-3
SON OF A DOPE FIEND 1-4
HEAVEN GOT A GHETTO 1&2
SKI MASK MONEY 1&2
By **Renta**

GORILLAZ IN THE BAY 1-4
TEARS OF A GANGSTA 1/&2
3X KRAZY 1&2
STRAIGHT BEAST MODE 1&2
By **DE'KARI**

TRIGGADALE 1-3
MURDA WAS THE CASE 1-3
By **Elijah R. Freeman**

SLAUGHTER GANG 1-3
RUTHLESS HEART 1-3
By **Willie Slaughter**

GOD BLESS THE TRAPPERS 1-3
THESE SCANDALOUS STREETS 1-3
FEAR MY GANGSTA 1-5
THESE STREETS DON'T LOVE NOBODY 1-2
BURY ME A G 1-5
A GANGSTA'S EMPIRE 1-4
THE DOPEMAN'S BODYGAURD 1&2
THE REALEST KILLAZ 1-3
THE LAST OF THE OGS 1-3
By **Tranay Adams**

MARRIED TO A BOSS 1-3
By **Destiny Skai & Chris Green**

CHRISTOPHER "DIESEL" HORNEZES

KINGZ OF THE GAME 1-7
CRIME BOSS 1-4
By **Playa Ray**

FUK SHYT
By **Blakk Diamond**

DON'T F#CK WITH MY HEART 1&2
By **Linnea**

ADDICTED TO THE DRAMA 1-3
IN THE ARM OF HIS BOSS
By **Jamila**

LOYALTY AIN'T PROMISED 1&2
By **Keith Williams**

YAYO 1-4
A SHOOTER'S AMBITION 1&2
BRED IN THE GAME
By **S. Allen**

TRAP GOD 1-3
RICH $AVAGE 1-3
MONEY IN THE GRAVE 1-3
CARTEL MONEY 1&2
By **Martell Troublesome Bolden**

FOREVER GANGSTA 1&2
GLOCKS ON SATIN SHEETS 1&2
By **Adrian Dulan**

TOE TAGZ 1-4
LEVELS TO THIS SHYT 1&2
IT'S JUST ME AND YOU
By **Ah'Million**

THE GIRLRILLA AND HER N*GGA KAY-O

KINGPIN DREAMS 1-3
RAN OFF ON DA PLUG
By **Paper Boi Rari**

THE STREETS MADE ME 1-3
By **Larry D. Wright**

CONFESSIONS OF A GANGSTA 1-4
CONFESSIONS OF A JACKBOY 1-3
CONFESSIONS OF A HITMAN
CONFESSIONS OF A DOPE BOY
By **Nicholas Lock**

I'M NOTHING WITHOUT HIS LOVE
SINS OF A THUG
TO THE THUG I LOVED BEFORE
A GANGSTA SAVED XMAS
IN A HUSTLER I TRUST
By **Monet Dragun**

QUIET MONEY 1-3
THUG LIFE 1-3
EXTENDED CLIP 1&2
A GANGSTA'S PARADISE
By **Trai'Quan**

CAUGHT UP IN THE LIFE 1-3
THE STREETS NEVER LET GO 1-3
By **Robert Baptiste**

NEW TO THE GAME 1-3
MONEY, MURDER & MEMORIES 1-3
By **Malik D. Rice**

CREAM 2-3
THE STREETS WILL TALK
By **Yolanda Moore**

CHRISTOPHER "DIESEL" HORNEZES

THE STREETS WILL NEVER CLOSE 1-3
By **K'ajji**

LIFE OF A SAVAGE 1-4
A GANGSTA'S QUR'AN 1-4
MURDA SEASON 1-3
GANGLAND CARTEL 1-3
CHI'RAQ GANGSTAS 1-4
KILLERS ON ELM STREET 1-3
JACK BOYZ N DA BRONX 1-3
A DOPEBOY'S DREAM 1-3
JACK BOYS VS DOPE BOYS 1-3
COKE GIRLZ
COKE BOYS
SOSA GANG 1&2
BRONX SAVAGES
BODYMORE KINGPINS
BLOOD OF A GOON
By **Romell Tukes**

CONCRETE KILLA 1-3
VICIOUS LOYALTY 1-3
BLOODY MONEY BAGS
By **Kingpen**

THE ULTIMATE SACRIFICE 1-6
KHADIFI
IF YOU CROSS ME ONCE 1-3
ANGEL 1-4
IN THE BLINK OF AN EYE
By **Anthony Fields**

THE LIFE OF A HOOD STAR
By **Ca$h & Rashia Wilson**

NIGHTMARES OF A HUSTLA 1-3
BLOOD AND GAMES 1&2
By **King Dream**

THE GIRLRILLA AND HER N*GGA KAY-O

CHRISTOPHER "DIESEL" HORNEZES

A GANGSTA'S KARMA 1-5
By **FLAME**

KING OF THE TRENCHES 1-3
By **GHOST & TRANAY ADAMS**

BAD BITCHES WIT GUNZ 1&2
PROBLEM SOLVED
By "Christopher Diesel" Hornezes

QUEEN OF THE ZOO 1&2
By **Black Migo**

GRIMEY WAYS 1-3
BETRAYAL OF A G
By **Ray Vinci**

XMAS WITH AN ATL SHOOTER
By **Ca$h & Destiny Skai**

KING KILLA 1&2
By **Vincent "Vitto" Holloway**

BETRAYAL OF A THUG 1&2
By **Fre$h**

COUNTDOWN OF A KILLA 1&2
SEX, MURDER AND GOD 1&2
GUNS DOWN, BOTTOMS UP 1&2
By Lo-Life

THE MURDER QUEENS 1-7
By **Michael Gallon**

FOR THE LOVE OF BLOOD 1-4
By **Jamel Mitchell**

THE GIRLRILLA AND HER N*GGA KAY-O

HOOD CONSIGLIERE 1&2
NO TIME FOR ERROR
By **Keese**

PROTÉGÉ OF A LEGEND 1,2&3
LOVE IN THE TRENCHES 1&2
By **Corey Robinson**

THE PLUG'S RUTHLESS DAUGHTER 1&2
By **Tony Daniels**

BORN IN THE GRAVE 1-3
CRIME PAYS
By **Self Made Tay**

MOAN IN MY MOUTH
By **XTASY**

TORN BETWEEN A GANGSTER AND A GENTLEMAN
By **J-BLUNT & Miss Kim**

LOYALTY IS EVERYTHING 1-3
CITY OF SMOKE 1-3
By **Molotti**

HERE TODAY GONE TOMORROW 1&2
By **Fly Rock**

WOMEN LIE MEN LIE 1-4
FIFTY SHADES OF SNOW 1-3
STACK BEFORE YOU SPLURGE
GIRLS FALL LIKE DOMINOES
NAÏVE TO THE STREETS
By **ROY MILLIGAN**

PILLOW PRINCESS
By **S. Hawkins**

CHRISTOPHER "DIESEL" HORNEZES

THE BUTTERFLY MAFIA 1-3
SALUTE MY SAVAGERY 1&2
By **Fumiya Payne**

THE LANE 1&2
By Ken-Ken Spence

THE PUSSY TRAP 1-5
By **Nene Capri**

DIRTY DNA
By **Blaque**

SANCTIFIED AND HORNY
by **XTASY**

BOOKS BY LDP'S CEO, CA$H

TRUST IN NO MAN
TRUST IN NO MAN 2
TRUST IN NO MAN 3
BONDED BY BLOOD
SHORTY GOT A THUG
THUGS CRY
THUGS CRY 2
THUGS CRY 3
TRUST NO BITCH
TRUST NO BITCH 2
TRUST NO BITCH 3
TIL MY CASKET DROPS
RESTRAINING ORDER
RESTRAINING ORDER 2
IN LOVE WITH A CONVICT
LIFE OF A HOOD STAR
XMAS WITH AN ATL SHOOTER

www.ingramcontent.com/pod-product-compliance
Lightning Source LLC
Chambersburg PA
CBHW071203260626
47162CB00003B/1149

* 9 7 8 1 9 6 5 4 4 8 9 9 1 *